Just a Cowboy's Secret Baby

Flyboys of Sweet Briar Ranch in North Dakota
Book Six
Jessie Gussman

Published By: Jessie Gussman

Contents

Acknowledgements

Cover art by Julia Gussman
Editing by Heather Hayden
Narration by Jay Dyess
Author Services by CE Author Assistant

Listen to a FREE professionally performed and produced audio-book version of this title on Youtube. Search for "Say With Jay" to browse all available FREE Dyess/Gussman audiobooks.

Chapter 1

Darby parked her car along the road, down the street from the only diner or place to get food in Sweet Water, North Dakota.

She wasn't sure whether this was a good idea or not, but she had committed, and now she was here.

"What are all those people doing standing around that store?" her daughter, Amber, asked from the back seat.

"I'm not sure. That's where I was planning on eating lunch, before we started looking around town."

"I'm hungry," Amber stated, which didn't surprise Darby. She was hungry too.

"Maybe they have some kind of sale going on or a popular recipe." She spoke, but mostly to herself. She hadn't heard or read of anything going on in Sweet Water today.

It was one in the afternoon. She wouldn't have expected a small-town diner to be so busy, but there were people milling around outside and looking in the windows. The door stood open, and a line snaked out. The odd thing about it was all the people moving around seemed to be women.

She might have thought maybe the local news station was holding an interview in the diner or some such thing like that, but that didn't explain why she didn't see any men around.

"Well, I guess we'll walk over and see if they're still selling lunch. And if not, I suppose we'll need to find somewhere else to eat." There wasn't any place else to eat in town, unless one counted the baked goods offered at the used bookstore. Eating was her excuse to linger, since she really had very little reason to be in town.

Well, it was a big reason to her.

She was looking for her daughter's father.

"Come on. Let's go see what we can find out." She opened her door, getting out and grabbing her purse.

Amber climbed out more slowly from the back seat. At eight years old, Amber wasn't quite old enough to understand that Darby wasn't just taking a joyride while on vacation. Although she knew Darby had sold her catering business and they were looking for a place to put down roots, as Darby had explained it to her.

She didn't know all the reasons why.

She also didn't know that the man who was her father lived in this town according to the information that Darby had been able to look up.

Which wasn't much.

He actually lived outside of town on a place called the Sweet Briar Ranch.

Darby was not familiar with North Dakota. She wasn't familiar with the West at all, being from Maryland.

She hadn't left Maryland for the sole purpose of finding Amber's father, but since she had to leave for Amber's sake, she thought she should look for Amber's father before she settled down anywhere else.

She didn't like the feeling of not having roots, of just drifting. She wanted to have a plan and live out her plan. She didn't want to just rely on God to show her the next step. She wanted to see the entire path from here to eternity.

That wasn't usually the way life worked out. And it definitely wasn't the way God usually worked. He wanted a person to take a step and then stand in faith until it was time to take another.

Sometimes the standing in faith was harder than taking steps.

"Mom?"

"Yes?" she said to her daughter absently.

"Is that...a woolly mammoth?"

Darby glanced at her daughter, bemused. North Dakota might be a little strange to them, but it wasn't like they had gone back in history.

She looked where Amber pointed, and her mouth dropped open.

"It does kind of look like one, doesn't it?" she asked, edging closer to her daughter and putting one hand in front of her as though to protect her.

"Do you think it's going to hurt us?"

"It's coming this way. I don't know if it's friendly. But a lot of times, animals will chase things that are running, so I don't want to run away."

They'd only walked a few yards from her car, but there was a bench on the sidewalk that was closer, so she walked, slowly and as carefully as she could in a state that was starting to feel a lot like panic, to the back of the bench and stood behind it, watching the animal draw closer.

"He looks friendly," Amber said.

"Yes, he does, doesn't he?"

It was true. What she could see of his eyes seemed calm and gentle, but she never took a risk when it came to her daughter.

"I don't think we should assume he is. You don't just go around petting strange cows." She thought it was a cow. She'd never seen one with quite that much...fur? Hair? She wasn't sure. But the horns he sported looked an awful lot like the horns on cows she'd read about in the Old West. Longhorns, they were called.

She didn't remember them having long, shaggy hair on them.

This one wasn't very tall. She'd always pictured longhorns as being much bigger.

The animal moseyed closer, stopping on the other side of the bench and seeming to look at them with those liquid gentle eyes.

Those horns were wicked.

Also, tigers had cute eyes, too. She'd looked at them often in the Baltimore Zoo and aquarium where she and Amber had spent many afternoons. They looked so cool, so sweet and cuddly.

They were wickedly dangerous.

There was no way she was going to assume that this beast in front of them was harmless, not with her daughter's life at stake.

"Mom, I think he wants us to pet him," Amber said, pulling at her hand, which Darby had gripped as she'd pulled her daughter behind the bench.

"Maybe he wants to eat us," Darby said, not in a scared tone but in a conversational tone. At least she hoped she kept the fear out of her voice

"Don't be silly, Mom. Cows eat grass."

"Maybe we've met the one cow in the entire United States who wants to expand his palate."

"Mother. You're being ridiculous."

Her daughter's vocabulary was much larger than a normal child's. That wasn't exactly the reason she'd left Maryland, but it was one of them. Her daughter had another special ability that had necessitated their flight from her home state.

"I'm just being a mom. I'm doing my job, which is to protect you. I don't know for sure whether this cow is dangerous or not, and those horns are huge. While you're almost certainly right that he's benign, if you're not correct, we have more to lose than if I am inaccurate in my observations of the situation."

"Mom, you talk like that when you're scared."

She was right. She had a tendency to be a lot more formal when she was trying to hide something, like fear, or anger, or frustration.

"I'm sorry. But while this beast seems to be harmless, we can't know for sure." She held on tight to her daughter's hand with one hand and made a shooing motion with her other hand. "Shoo. Go on. Get out of here."

The animal looked at them, then shook its head.

Darby jumped back, yanking her daughter with her.

She almost felt foolish, but then the animal looked at them, stretched out its neck, and made the biggest, most ghastly, and frightening noise that Darby had ever heard.

It felt like her eardrums were going to burst.

She grabbed her child more closely to her, hugging her next to her side while keeping both of her frightened eyes on the beast in front of her.

"I'm sorry, ma'am. I'm assuming this car with the out of state tags is yours. Billy here must have noticed we had someone new in town and came to welcome you folks to North Dakota."

A man, dressed in cowboy boots, worn blue jeans, a belt buckle as big as Texas right in the center of his belly, and a button-down shirt with the top two buttons unbuttoned and the sleeves rolled up to the elbows, spoke behind her. Completing his ensemble was a cowboy hat that hid half the man's face. She couldn't quite see what color his eyes were, but the jaw that stuck out from underneath it was covered in stubble and looked to be square and hard.

"Billy?"

"That's our steer." The man's voice held humor. A shiver traveled up her spine. "Sweet Water's own mascot. He doesn't usually welcome strangers. In fact, he usually shies away. But I guess he saw you coming and figured your daughter here would love to pet him."

The man grinned at Amber, who grinned back up at him.

"Really? You mean I could really pet him?"

"Sure can. He's gentle as a lamb. As long as your mom says it's okay."

"Are you sure?"

"Sure as shooting. When the town has festivals, which is pretty much every other week, Billy always gets rounded up and put in a makeshift petting zoo and the kids sit on his back, hang on his horns, and crawl over him. He loves it."

"That's crazy," she couldn't help but say.

"I think, if you're actually from Maryland, and this is your first time in North Dakota, that's going to look pretty normal once you see the rest of the stuff these North Dakota folks do."

"You're talking like you aren't from North Dakota, and yet you sound like you are," she said, noticing the way he interchanged his third- and first-person pronouns.

"I've lived here for not quite two years, and I got acclimated pretty well. And by that, I mean that I survived two winters and feel like I should earn some kind of major award for that."

She laughed. "That's the sign that you've acclimated to the state? Surviving the winter?"

"I don't know how long you're staying, but if you're here in January, you'll feel like you need a badge of honor too if you make it through the month."

"I'm not sure if we're staying or not," Darby said, liking this man, who told it like it was and who seemed friendly but not in her face, gave her enough space to make her feel comfortable.

"Mom, can I pet the cow?"

"It's actually a steer," the man corrected Amber. She liked that he didn't treat her like a little kid but acted like she was capable of rational thought.

So many men didn't know how to act around children.

"I suppose if the man... I guess we should introduce ourselves," she said a little uncertainly. She wasn't used to meeting strange men on the street and handing out her name like candy. But Sweet Water seemed like a friendly place and a lot different from Baltimore. Plus, the man had been kind.

That didn't mean she trusted him. It just meant she was going to introduce herself.

"I'm Darby, this is my daughter, Amber." She held out her hand.

The man took it. His hands were rough, strong, and his grip firm. "I'm Jonah Mills."

Darby gasped.

Her train of thought was a little derailed because she wasn't expecting his grip to make jolts of electricity shoot up her arm. Unexpected, but not unpleasant.

As he stepped a little closer, she could see under the brim of his hat to the deep brown eyes shadowed there. Serious, but with laugh lines crinkling the corners.

Her eyes caught on his, and their hands remain clasped even after they stopped pumping.

This was the man. Amber's father.

Her shock was still great, her complete surprise at...not just finding the man, and finding him the moment she got into the town, but that she would feel...whatever it was that she felt while touching him. An odd sensation, and even odder when combined with her inability to tear her eyes away from his.

"Mom! Are you gonna let him help me pet Billy?" Amber's voice broke into her consciousness, and she couldn't believe she'd almost forgotten she had a daughter, let alone that they were standing on a street in the middle of a North Dakota town, and there were other people in the world.

She yanked her hand away, embarrassed, backing up. "Of course. He said it was okay, just be careful."

The man, Jonah, seemed to look at her, study her, for another few moments that felt like a really long time before he turned to Amber with an easy grin on his face. "You can come on around the other side of the bench. I promise you, Billy is as tame as an animal gets. He loves attention."

Amber went around, standing trustingly beside Jonah as she followed his example and put her hand on the steer's fur.

"In Sweet Water, we like to think that Billy is a bit of a matchmaker. He's had a hand in getting several local couples together and has started to get himself quite a reputation. Local legend has it that Billy is the way he is because he has an unrequited love for the town pig, Munchy. Munchy doesn't want to have anything to do with Billy, so in order for Billy to feel better about himself, he helps other people who are looking for love get together."

Darby laughed and rolled her eyes at the silliness of Western towns. "Sounds to me like Sweet Water's desperate for tourism dollars."

"Well, that's the funny thing, we haven't really announced it to the outside world. Only people here in Sweet Water get to find out about Billy the steer who thinks he's Cupid."

"Maybe you're right about those North Dakota winters, and they kind of make people a little crazy in the head." She spoke, hoping her voice sounded a little bit reasonable.

She hadn't really gotten off on a very good foot with this man, and she was here hoping to have a working relationship with him. But she just couldn't let the idea of a steer who wanted people to find love go without making fun of it just a little.

"Laugh if you want to. There are several people in town who are married because of this old boy," Jonah said, petting him. He looked over his shoulder at her. "You can come on over and give him a pat if you want to."

Darby wasn't very interested in petting the steer, but she always tried to lead by example with her daughter, and while her daughter was already scratching the animal like she'd been doing it for years, Darby thought it would be best for her to do it as well, just to let her daughter know that it was good to not give in to your fear.

Chapter 2

"**S**o how does the steer go about matching couples together?" Darby asked, unable to keep the bit of sarcasm out of her voice as she walked over, petting the brown fur which was surprisingly soft.

"Well, I've heard of him doing it several different ways," Jonah began. "In one case, he ran into a woman and knocked her into the arms of her potential husband."

"I thought you said he was safe?" Darby asked, freezing and looking again at the steer who seemed to be in some kind of cow heaven, with his eyes closed, his head stretched out, and three sets of hands on him.

To be honest, it was kind of hard for her to picture him running into anyone and knocking them down. Or doing any kind of damage to anyone.

"Yes. He's never done that to anyone except when he seems to be doing his matchmaking. Then, all bets are off. But I'm pretty sure Amber here is safe. He hasn't tried to match anyone under the age of twenty-five so far."

"So now you're telling me he knows people's ages, as well as whether or not they're looking for love?" Darby asked, brows raised but both hands back scratching the bovine.

"That's what it seems like," Jonah said.

"Was the woman hurt?" she asked.

"Nope. In one instance, her potential husband caught her. In another instance, he dropped her, but the results have been the same. I think once he knocked the suitor and his potential love interest down on the sidewalk. That was my good friend Elias. He just got married late last fall, and they're expecting their first little one together this summer. They own the diner."

He jerked his head across the street, which drew Darby's attention away from the steer and reminded her that they hadn't eaten.

"What's going on at the diner?" Darby asked, seeing it was just as crowded as it had been.

"That is something people in Sweet Water are trying to do to get themselves on the map."

"I knew it. Those big tourism dollar signs are so tempting."

"I don't know if it's dollars so much as it's just a bunch of old men who are looking for something to entertain themselves in their golden years."

"A bunch of old men? I thought you said your friend and his wife own the diner."

"Yes, but the old men are looking for a woman who can cook to join them on their TikTok channel. They're hoping to make videos that go viral and make money. Although, I really think it's just something to keep them entertained. It keeps the town entertained too. Especially on the long winter days when, like you surmised, we're looking for things to entertain ourselves with."

"I figured," Darby said, grinning. Winters were usually pretty mild in Maryland, although they did get occasional snow and ice, even some days of freezing temperatures. Enough to make her long for warmer weather so she could go outside and get around without worrying about tripping, slipping and falling, or getting her car stuck in a snowdrift.

"I guess when I saw you, I figured that's what you were here for, but I thought I'd better rescue you from Billy, since you seemed to be stuck behind the bench."

"Oh. No. We're not here for that."

"Oh? You're here for something else?" he asked, and it seemed like an innocent question. Something that people in small towns would ask without a second thought. But she failed to be casual as she stumbled over her answer.

"I... I... I just sold my business in Maryland, and I'm looking for a job."

"Really?" Jonah said, looking at her with interest. "People don't usually show up in Sweet Water when they're conducting a job search."

"No. I guess they probably don't."

She'd been caught. Although she'd been telling the truth, it wasn't quite the whole truth, and for some reason, God never let her get away with that. It was a little frustrating, because it seemed like it was something the rest of the world could do.

"What kind of business did you have?"

"It was just a small business," she said, rather evasively.

It wasn't that she didn't want him to know she had a catering business, she just wasn't always comfortable giving out a whole bunch of details to someone that she didn't know. And while this was the man that she wanted to be around, she didn't want him to know that she'd sold the business for a tidy profit and didn't really need to work. Not for a while anyway. Although, she had planned to find a place to stay and a job so she could put some of the money in a college fund for Amber. Or maybe it would finance some of the trips they might take because of her special talent.

As though he could sense her discomfort, Jonah said, "I was just asking because my buddies and I own a ranch. We're all former Air Force, and we own a crop-dusting service. We've been hitting the pavement pretty hard trying to drum up clients last fall and winter, and we actually have a full schedule of work starting in a couple of weeks, going through October. We're looking for someone to keep the books and also cook and clean and do laundry when we manage to make it home. There's going to be equipment to fix and maintain, and in the short time we're back between jobs, we've been discussing it would be easier to hire someone to help with the household things and keep us on schedule. If we can find someone who can do all of that."

After saying she was looking for a job, she could hardly tell him she wasn't interested. To be honest, there was a part of her that got excited. After all, this was the man she wanted to be around, and what better way to do it than by working for him?

The thing was, she'd been planning on telling him right away about his daughter, but... She wasn't sure how she didn't realize when she started out that it was going to be so difficult to just drop a bomb like that on someone.

"I did do my own paperwork for my business, and I'm definitely familiar with scheduling software." She smiled. "I do know how to do laundry, too. The business I owned was a catering company, so I suppose I can cook fairly well also."

He laughed. "Sounds like a perfect fit if you can use a washing machine."

"I can use the washer just fine, it's the dryer I sometimes have trouble with." She was mostly joking, and he seemed to realize that because he looked at her with the dimple on his face winking at her.

It made him look endearing, and she again had trouble trying to pull her eyes away.

She had never in a million years expected Amber's father to be someone she was attracted to. But she was thinking that must be what this feeling was. The feeling of getting lost in his eyes and wanting to step closer.

Trying to gather her thoughts, she forced herself to think.

She hadn't wanted to announce to him her real reason for being there, not in front of Amber.

But if she succeeded in securing this job where she would see him on a regular basis, she would almost certainly be able to find a good time.

"I'm definitely interested. We...don't have a place to stay, though. So, I have to see if I can work something out with that."

"We actually have an extra bedroom in the farmhouse, if you're comfortable with that."

"I think I would be. On a temporary basis. Amber will need her own room at some point, but I think if I would be staying at a farmhouse with a bunch of men, I would feel better if she were sleeping with me anyway." She wasn't sure if it was safe to accept a job where she was staying with men she didn't know, even if one of them was the father of her child.

Somehow it made her feel a little better to know they were all former military men, but that didn't always mean what it somehow seemed.

"Is there a good lock on the door?"

"I can make sure there is."

"What's up, guys?" a male voice said, causing Darby to startle and turn.

"I think I might have found us a solution to our problems," Jonah said, and Darby grinned a little. She was hardly the solution to his problems.

"You mean you found a higher force?" the man asked, looking at Darby, his eyes running to Amber, before going back to Darby.

Then he froze, and his eyes went back to Amber.

Oh, no. Surely this man hadn't seen any kind of resemblance between Amber and Jonah.

She hadn't gotten a good look at Jonah's eyes, other than they were brown and very magnetic. Actually, she *had* gotten a good look at his eyes, but she'd been so busy thinking about the way his eyes made her feel that she hadn't thought to notice they actually were the exact same color as Amber's.

But Jonah's friend should have no reason to suspect that Jonah had a child. After all, no one had ever told him.

"I'm Gideon," the man said, holding out his hand.

"I'm Darby. This is my daughter, Amber."

"And you're new in town?"

"Yes. This is my first time in Sweet Water."

"You and Jonah were talking like you knew each other. Is this an old friend?" he asked, lifting his eyes to his buddy.

"This is my first time meeting her," Jonah said with a shake of his head.

"I see." Gideon waved a hand back at the busy diner. "I assume she's here to audition for the three men and a lady."

"No. She's actually here looking for a job."

"That's a job."

"It probably isn't going to pay anything," Jonah pointed out.

Gideon eyed Darby. Not in a way that made her uncomfortable, but in a way that made her want to laugh and strike a pose.

He lifted a brow. "She looks cute and not quite as eager as the other ladies that are clamoring for attention. I bet the old men would consider her."

"Did you not hear me? She already has a job. We're hiring her." Jonah's words were a little more forceful than they needed to be. She hadn't actually said she would do the job. And he hadn't actually hired her.

They'd just expressed a mutual interest.

"She can do both. It's not like the old coots are going to take that much time. And it might be fun for her. I bet the men didn't even consider that it might be good to have a lady *and* a daughter." He tilted his head to the side. "Although a lady and a baby would be much better."

"Did you miss what I just said? She's going to work for us."

Darby could have stepped in, but she'd been fascinated by listening to them and wanted to see where the conversation was going to go.

"She can work for them too." Gideon grinned engagingly at Darby. "How about you come with me? I'll take you in the back door. I have an in with the boss men. I just might be able to put in a good word for you."

"Gideon. She's not interested."

Maybe it was Jonah insisting that she wasn't interested, or maybe it was something in the tone of his voice. But something made her want to do the exact opposite of whatever it was that he said.

"Maybe I am."

"See? I told you she was," Gideon said, taking a hold of her elbow and saying to Amber, "Come on. Let's go see how your mom does with these old fellows. I bet she can hold her own with them. They can be kind of overpowering, but your mom seems like a lady who can handle herself."

Amber grinned at him and took his hand without him even offering it. Gideon was definitely a charismatic man.

"Mom can hold her own. She can be pretty ferocious when she wants to be. Most of the time, she's pretty easygoing. In fact, I can get whatever I want a lot of times. I just have to ask in the right way."

That was news to Darby.

She spoke to her daughter. "When has that happened?" she asked, exaggerating her offense so it almost sounded like humor.

"All the time. You're a pushover."

"Just because I'm nice does not mean I'm a pushover."

"Mom, trust me. You need to be much firmer. I need a man's hand to make sure that I don't get out of line. I think you need to give this a try."

She snapped her mouth closed. A man's hand? She wanted to ask where that came from, but Gideon was already laughing, and she could hear Jonah's chuckle even though he trailed behind them, following them across the street.

Amber had no idea they were in Sweet Water to find her dad. At least, Darby didn't think so. She was a smart kid. Too smart. Maybe she'd figured it out.

As they crossed the street, she tried to remember what exactly she had told her daughter. Amber was very astute and understood a lot more than what a child of eight was expected to.

By the time they crossed the street, Jonah had caught up with her and walked by her side.

"Don't let Gideon strong-arm you into anything. This might not be something you're interested in," he said, low, almost as though Gideon wouldn't be able to hear him, but she would.

"Stop trying to talk her out of it before she's even seen what's going on. I took one look at her and figured she was perfect for the job."

"She's perfect for the job at our ranch," Jonah said, his voice sounding insistent.

"She would be perfect for that too, but did you hear me say that she could do both?"

"Is there a reason you don't want me to do both?" Darby asked, turning to look at Jonah. She really didn't want to get on his bad side. Not that she was afraid of him or anything, but she wanted to have a good relationship with him. Hopefully, if things worked out, they would be sharing, if not custody of Amber, at least Jonah would be in her life in some way.

Darby wasn't out for money. She had plenty of that, but she was out for someone to help her protect Amber.

Once people realized her gift, they wanted to take her childhood away and force her to work on what she was good at beyond all else.

Darby believed in hard work, and she also believed in children working, but she really couldn't name a person who had been famous as a child, who had been happy about that as an adult. Who didn't think at least some of their childhood had been robbed from them.

She knew she was walking a tightrope, because she wanted Amber to be able to develop her skills, but she also didn't want Amber to lose the happy innocence that she still had. That was the main reason for looking for Jonah.

That, and it didn't seem right for a man to not know he was a father and have the opportunity to be a dad to his daughter. Especially a daughter as wonderful as Amber.

So far, she had no reason to doubt that he would be totally with her on her quest to protect Amber.

But while she wanted to respect his wishes, she thought that whatever Gideon was up to was harmless fun and maybe exactly what she needed—after all, she wanted Amber to have a fun childhood and enjoy different experiences. If they were doing some kind of cooking thing on TikTok, it wouldn't have anything to do with what Amber was skilled in. If she did decide to follow her talent, she would have something completely different to do that would relax her and allow her to unwind.

Not that an eight-year-old should ever have to be pushed so hard that she would have to relax and unwind.

Darby cringed just thinking about it.

"Come back through here, and we'll go in the back door. The men are doing auditions, but they're getting frustrated, because no one seems to be working out."

Aware of Jonah's glower beside her, she held tight to Amber's hand and went back between the buildings, knowing the plan she had set in motion had somehow spiraled out of her control, and she had no idea what was going to come next.

Chapter 3

J onah trailed along behind Gideon and the woman and her
daughter.

Darby.

That wasn't a common name, and he didn't think he'd ever heard
of anyone named that before.

But the woman had struck him.

He couldn't exactly explain how, but he had this desire to be
closer to her. To know her better. To stay with her.

Normally, he didn't mind Gideon coming along and taking control, especially when it had to do with people.

Gideon was much more of a people person than he was.

Funny, now that Gideon was with this woman, he wasn't limping
at all on the leg he'd broken when he'd fallen on ice back at the
beginning of November.

He'd been in a cast for a while and had just recently been cleared
to resume normal activities.

It had been a complicated break and had laid him up all winter.

Gideon had milked it out, in typical Gideon fashion.

Still, all of a sudden, his leg didn't seem to bother him at all, and
it made Jonah wonder if he'd been putting on a show all winter. Or
if he just didn't want to seem weak in front of Darby.

Or, knowing Gideon, he might have sensed Jonah's interest and
just wanted to rile him.

Jonah determined he wouldn't get upset. Darby was intriguing,
but he could push her out of his mind. Although the little girl

had seemed familiar. Not in a nostalgic way, just in a way like she reminded him of someone he knew.

He hadn't quite put his finger on who, but someone.

Regardless, he felt it was more important to nail down the fact that the woman would be working for them on their ranch rather than getting her involved with the old coots.

Gideon seemed to have taken the exact opposite approach, and Jonah wished he could take him aside to figure out why. And, at the same time, talk some sense into him. Because they should be working on getting things set up for their farm and business and not worried about helping the old men find someone for their TikTok channel. There were plenty of women milling around the diner. The men would find someone with or without them.

That was just like Gideon, always doing frivolous things rather than the things that needed to be done.

Of course, talking about frivolous, Jonah had launched into an explanation of Billy and his matchmaking abilities when he first met the woman.

He'd wanted to tease her and ask her if she was looking for a husband, because Billy could find her one.

He'd noticed that she had no ring on her hand, even though he'd assumed that the girl who was with her was her daughter.

She was protective like a mother.

But the idea of the woman finding love with someone else, even though he'd just met her, had hit him the wrong way, and he didn't want to even joke about it.

Odd that it meant so much to him.

Normally he didn't care.

He'd been married once, and that had been enough to teach him that women weren't always what they seemed. A lot of times, when the social mask came off, they were not kind or gentle or loving.

Quite the opposite.

And vindictive as well.

He'd experienced that quite enough.

Of course, as he'd grown older, he'd realized that not all women were like that. Some of his buddies had gotten married and seemed happy. In fact, it seemed like they really loved their wives and that their wives were kind and sincere people.

Not the split personality that his wife seemed to have.

Funny that he hadn't talked to Nora or thought about her in years.

Other than a moment or two in passing relief that he wasn't married anymore.

She had certainly never looked out for him. He hadn't felt like he had a companion or friend even. It felt more like he was constantly doing the wrong thing and being berated for things he didn't even realize that he messed up on.

There was no grace or love or forgiveness.

It was all about him doing things wrong and needing to apologize and make it up to her.

He was glad she walked out. He couldn't imagine spending the rest of his life trying to make up to her whatever perceived slight she accused him of daily.

They walked around the back of the building, through the spot where the townspeople fed Billy and Munchie.

Billy hadn't followed them, which Jonah thought was a little odd.

After all, they were heading to where the steer normally ate.

One would have thought he would have come along, hoping for a meal.

Even though he'd been talking kind of whimsically to Darby about the steer, everything he said had been true.

Maybe the steer planned on matchmaking between Darby and Gideon.

Just as he thought that, their laughter floated back in the air to him and grated on his nerves.

He didn't want to have to witness a romance between the two of them. Maybe it would be better if Darby didn't work for them. If Gideon and she got together, he wasn't sure he would be able to stand to watch it day after day.

Although Amber was cute. Maybe he and Amber could go on horseback rides while Gideon and Darby courted.

That still didn't sit well with him, but he couldn't put a finger on why.

They got to the door, and Gideon opened it, holding it for Darby and Amber and then walking in front of Jonah.

Jonah almost laughed, since Gideon was being so obvious. He wanted to lay claim to Darby, and it irritated Jonah that her loyalty was so light that she would go from talking to Jonah to running around with Gideon.

Just as he thought that, Darby looked around until her eyes met his.

"I don't know what this job entails or if it will amount to anything, but it got me in the diner, and Amber and I are starving."

"Why didn't you just say so? I could have made sure you got in the diner."

"You didn't offer."

"I didn't know."

"I just told you. So, I'm going along with this, because it sounds like fun, but...I haven't forgotten you offered me a job first."

He couldn't help it. He appreciated loyalty and admired it in people. That did a lot for raising his estimation of this woman. Of course, it didn't help the strange attraction he couldn't quite define.

"If you're interested, the job is yours. We're not a big company, and we don't get fancy."

"All right then. Whatever happens now, I'll make sure that they know that I already have a job. Full-time hours?"

"Full-time hours, and you have a bedroom, and..." He named an hourly wage.

"That's more than fair."

"It's what we agreed on. We just haven't gotten around to advertising the job yet. We didn't want just anyone."

He almost laughed when he said that, because he'd just offered the job to someone he hadn't even done a background check on.

For all he knew, the girl she was leading around could be kidnapped.

He hardly thought so. She protected the little girl like a mother should, and the girl clung to her, unafraid.

She seemed like a smart little thing, too.

Darby turned back to where Gideon was talking to someone in the kitchen doorway.

After a few minutes, Gideon turned around.

"Miss Jane said you guys can go upstairs to her apartment, and the old fellas will be up. That will save you fighting the crowd in the diner."

"In the meantime, I'll make sure you get some food brought up. Is there anything in particular you can't eat? Or something you want?"

"We're not allergic to anything, but a drink and some food would be lovely."

"I'll bring you their chicken. It's—" He almost told her the name of the chicken.

For some reason, he held off. There wasn't any truth to the rumors that the chicken had any kind of romantic abilities, but it seemed like the woman set foot in their town, and before he barely met her, he was talking about a matchmaking steer, and then if he mentioned the Marry Me Chicken... That would be enough to send him running in the opposite direction if he pulled into a town and that happened to him.

He didn't want her to run away, so he finished his sentence, ignoring the awkward pause. "—a chicken dish that is very popular here in town. They even pack it up and mail it to people who order online."

"Wow. It's that famous?" Her brows raised, like she couldn't believe a place as small as Sweet Water could be famous outside of the town, let alone be known so far away that they'd need to mail anything out.

"Wait until we bring it to you and you taste it, then you can tell me whether it's worth it or not."

Gideon slapped his back. "All right, old buddy. You go get food, and I'll continue to play agent to this lovely woman and her daughter." He sounded a little sarcastic, like he was irritated with Jonah.

He didn't usually butt in when Gideon took over. Gideon was the outgoing extrovert who loved to talk to people and was a bit of a flirt.

He enjoyed laughing and joking and talking, whereas Jonah was quieter and had a tendency to move along the periphery of a crowd.

He supposed it was quite odd for him to be still involved in any conversation where Gideon had taken over. But he couldn't seem to help himself where Darby was concerned.

The idea that she and her daughter were hungry and needed food seemed to be of the utmost importance in his mind.

Maybe that was because the question of her employment was settled, and he knew she would be spending more time with him. Living in the same house. Although, with other people there including her daughter, so he didn't see it as an inappropriate thing.

As long as they weren't in a relationship.

His buddies had discussed it, and they decided that that was best—offer a room as a part of the employment package.

In his mind, he pictured an older lady, a grandmotherly type perhaps, someone in her fifties, taking over. He hadn't expected someone quite as young as Darby, who was maybe in her early thirties. Not that he was any great judge of people's ages.

He went into the kitchen, where Peter, the cook, was working diligently, and Elias, Jonah's former commander, had just walked in to grab an order.

"I need two orders of chicken and two drinks, for a woman who's upstairs in your apartment."

"Is that the one that the old men are going to go talk to?" Elias asked, and it didn't surprise Jonah that the information had already gotten passed around.

Small towns were notorious for the speed of transmission of info, especially about people.

"That's the one. Are they on their way up?"

"Yeah. They're in the process of telling the folks that are waiting that they're taking a lunch break."

"Have they found anyone?" Jonah asked, hoping he didn't sound too hopeful. Gideon had somehow managed to disappear and was most likely trying to bias the opinion of the men toward Darby, since he, for some reason, really seemed to want her to get that job.

"No. I think they're being a little picky. But they just haven't found anyone who 'feels right.'" Elias shook his head and laughed. "They're worse than a bunch of women."

He didn't say anything more about that but told Peter to dish up two helpings of chicken and told Jonah that he'd be back with two drinks. Then he grabbed his orders and walked back out.

"Get me two bowls from there," Peter said, nodding his head toward a stack of clean dishes.

Jonah obeyed, bringing the bowls over to where Peter had the chicken in a pot warming on the stove.

"I don't know, but if I were you and I wasn't planning on getting married, I might get someone else to carry this stuff up. It's pretty potent."

"Potent?"

"Unless you're looking for that woman to fall in love with you, I'd send it up with your buddy Gideon. You don't look like the kind of guy who'd be interested in a girl. But I can tell you, this stuff hasn't failed to work yet."

"Thanks for the warning. I bet I'll be immune."

"You're not who I'm worried about."

"I hardly think she's going to have any problems resisting me. I'm not exactly the most engaging and appealing man the world has ever seen."

It had never bothered him either. He didn't want to be the center of attention. Didn't want every eye on him and wasn't trying to catch any woman's eye.

"I don't think it works like that. It doesn't cause love to act the way we normally think of it. It doesn't matter what you look like."

"I'll take your word for it," he said, picking up the bowls Peter had dished out. "Tell Elias I'll be back down for the drinks." He didn't want Gideon to get the chicken and carry it up. If it truly made people fall in love...he wasn't sure why, but the idea that Gideon and Darby might get together just rubbed him the wrong way. He'd rather it was him.

Whoa.

Was that true?

Chapter 4

J onah didn't want to face the thought that he wanted Gideon out of the picture where Darby was concerned, so he pushed it aside, telling himself, if the old men were on the way up, he wanted Darby and Amber to be able to eat before they started being interrogated.

Mr. Marshall, Mr. Blaze, and Mr. Junior could be rather...not intimidating, because they were nice old guys, but...overwhelming.

Darby would do better facing them on a full stomach. That's what he told himself, anyway.

And while he was up there, maybe Jonah would give her a little warning about them.

"Just remember what I said. Brace yourself, because it's on its way."

Jonah laughed, assuming Peter was kidding, and walked out holding the chicken.

He went up the stairs, and since he didn't have a hand, he used one of the bowls to gently tap on the door.

It opened immediately like Darby had been standing beside it, uncertain of what to do.

He stepped in, using his elbow to close the door behind him.

Darby clasped her hands together in front of her and stood, still looking unsure.

He took pity on her and tried to put her at ease. "Maybe where you come from, this is kind of unusual, but around here, if someone tells you to go into their home and make yourself at home, they really mean it."

"All right. It was just a little bit weird to go into somebody's house and just walk in."

"I promise you, if there'd been any problems with it at all, they wouldn't have told you to do it. But that's just kind of the way we roll around here."

"You talk funny," Amber said from where she had wandered over to the kitchen table. She hadn't sat down, but she kind of hung there, like she was uncertain as well.

"Amber, it's not polite to tell people they talk funny," Darby reprimanded her daughter.

"It's okay. She's probably right."

"You already said you're not originally from here? I don't think you mentioned where you're from? Not from the South."

"I'm not sure if I did or not, but you're right. I'm originally from Indiana. I joined the Air Force, and that has a way of shuffling a guy around. I've been to a bunch of different states, a couple different countries, and North Dakota is where I ended up with some of my buddies."

She had her mouth open, almost as though she wanted to ask him something else, but she didn't, as he put the bowls on the table and then went over to the counter and started rummaging through drawers to find the silverware.

That's exactly what Jonah would do in his home, and he didn't have any qualms about doing it in his friend's.

After all, like he'd just told her, they wouldn't have sent her up if they hadn't intended for her to make herself at home.

Grabbing two spoons, he turned, intending to hand them to Darby and Amber, but they had their heads bowed and Darby was saying a soft prayer.

That picture, of the two bent heads sitting at a table with steaming bowls of chicken in front of them, just a humble home, an unpretentious picture, but one that stirred something in his heart.

Something about home and hearth and family. Something old-fashioned and sweet. Something about bygone days and values that seemed to be disappearing faster than ice on the sidewalk in July.

He didn't say anything once they were done, just set the spoons down in front of them, and then he said, "I'll be right back. Elias was getting your drinks. That's the man who lives here with his wife, Jane, and their two girls."

"They're the ones who own the diner?" Darby asked.

"That's right."

"Would you please tell them thank you if you see them?"

"I will." He paused. "Eat quickly. You're gonna want that fortification because the old guys are on their way up. They were sending everyone else away and saying they were taking a lunch break, and if I know Gideon, he was putting a lot of bugs in their ear about how they should hire you."

"So you think this is a sure thing?" she asked with her brow raised, seeming to not know whether to be horrified or amused.

"Actually, probably not. These old guys have minds of their own, opinions that sometimes are way out there, and they aren't going to let someone else tell them how to run their channel. Even if they don't actually have it up and running."

"Oh really?"

"From my understanding, they do have several viral videos, but it was their last atrocity that garnered all this attention, and I'm not sure they like it."

"I don't know anyone who would. It seemed like a madhouse down there."

"You should have been inside the dining room area. It was crazy. It was almost like the guys were celebrities. And from one video.

I was a little bit concerned that things were not going to stay safe, but Elias can be pretty intimidating, and he kept things in order. Somehow, they still managed to feed their patrons too. But you saw how difficult it was to get in."

She nodded, and he figured he should leave so she and her daughter could eat and maybe chat a little.

What an initiation to their small town. To be practically dragged off the street and offered two different jobs in the space of thirty minutes.

Having people almost fight over you.

As he put his hand on the doorknob ready to go out, he felt compelled to say, "Sweet Water is not usually like this. We're a pretty unpretentious, calm, and quiet town."

"So you say." Darby took her spoon and pointed to the bowl. "This wouldn't happen to be the world-famous Sweet Water Marry Me Chicken, would it?"

He realized she must have been on her phone while he was gone. "It is."

"Interesting."

That's all she said before she looked back down at her bowl and took another bite.

She didn't seem upset, but he felt like he had to explain. "I was going to tell you, but I already talked about Billy and his matchmaking abilities, and I figured if I talked about the Marry Me Chicken, you would think I was going a little over the top and get the wrong impression."

"Oh no. I don't think I got the wrong impression at all," Darby said, sounding a little mysterious.

He wasn't sure exactly what she meant by that. He supposed it didn't matter.

He left, and by the time he got down and got the drinks, the old men were tripping through the kitchen, on their way up the stairs. He ended up following them, wishing he'd been a little quicker, because Darby might want to drink before she had to deal with them.

"I don't understand why Gideon was so all fired set on this woman. We haven't found anyone else who looks the slightest bit good for the job," Marshall mumbled as he went up the stairs, one painful step at a time.

"Why do we have to talk to her up here? There's like a million stairs, and I'm lucky if I can do three at a time without taking a half an hour break." Junior said, huffing and puffing up after him.

"Would you guys stop your confounded complaining? It's annoying to always be around people who are never satisfied with anything. There were fifty ladies we interviewed that would have been fine for the job. One of you two had a problem with every one, and we had to say no to all of them," Blaze mumbled, causing Jonah to smile.

It sounded like Blaze had fallen in love with every woman they'd interviewed.

Sometimes he wished he could be like that. Just open and trusting in his personality and having an easy-come, easy-go attitude.

He was anything but. It took him a while to trust people, at least it usually did. Darby seemed to be the exception. Still, he didn't feel completely comfortable with her. Not like Gideon did, talking easily about everything.

It was just as well, because once he warmed up to someone, he hated letting them go.

The men finally made it to the top of the stairs and walked in. Jonah followed them in, closing the door and putting the drinks down on the table.

He knew he should probably leave. He hadn't sat in on any other interviews.

Still, he backed off, moving to stand by the door, but he decided that he'd just stand watch, unless they asked him to leave. He couldn't explain why and didn't try to figure it out. Just stood, content to watch and listen.

Chapter 5

"So you're the lady that we're not going to be able to resist?" the first old fellow through the door said as he made it into the kitchen, huffing and puffing.

"Whoa," Darby said, holding one hand up. "I didn't say that. In fact, I wasn't here to audition for whatever it is that you guys have. The TikTok thing or whatever."

"You're not?" the second man said, sounding surprised.

"No. I wasn't. I didn't know anything about it."

"Then...what were you doing in town?"

Darby paused. She couldn't help it. She was a terrible liar, and she felt like she'd be lying if she didn't give the main reason she'd been there. "I need a job."

"That's just perfect. We can hire you."

She wanted to be honest, so as they sat back down, she said, "I didn't know that you were hiring. I stopped to get a bite to eat at the diner, but it was full."

"We had no idea things were going to get so crazy," the first man said, holding out his hand. "I'm Marshall, and it's good to meet you." She shook his hand and was about to say it was nice to meet him, when he said in a stage whisper over his shoulder, "I think this is the one."

Darby heard him just fine, and she wasn't sure whether he was doing that to put her at ease or just to let his friends know that he approved.

Regardless, the second man came over and shook her hand. "I'm Blaze. And I'm pleased to meet you."

"I'm pleased to meet you, too, Mr. Blaze. This is my daughter, Amber," she said, nodding at Amber who smiled and gave a little wave, but didn't say anything because her mouth was full of chicken.

Darby had to admit that it truly was the best chicken she'd ever had. She could see why it was so famous. She'd never had anything quite like it, and it would definitely go down in her book as one of the top three meals she'd ever had, which was kind of interesting considering her humble surroundings here.

"And I'm Junior," the third man said, shaking her hand. They all filed around the table and found chairs, sitting down.

It made Darby want to stop eating, but there was something about the chicken that wouldn't let her quit, and she figured it wouldn't hurt if she ate while she talked to them.

"So you aren't here because of the video?"

"What video?"

"The video that went viral on TikTok?"

"I just got on TikTok to try to look you guys up, and I saw a video with…" She narrowed her eyes, trying to figure out which one of the men had been on the video. She pointed to the one who'd introduced himself as Marshall. "I think it was you. Just saying who you are and that you wanted a lady. Is that the one that went viral?"

"We had a lot of success with that one, but it's not the reason that we have so many people hanging around here today."

"Oh?" she asked, surprised. She hadn't had time to see any more videos, but she supposed she shouldn't be surprised, because that video had been very plain. Of course, she had no idea of what would make a video go viral.

"Yeah. We did another video, with me holding a sign up with our address on it. In the first video, people kept asking us where we were from, and we got tired of typing our address in over and over in the comments, plus the girls told us that wasn't a good practice."

"So, we made a second video with the sign."

"Oh. And that was you?" she said to the man who introduced himself as Junior.

"Yep. It was me. Personally, I think my video was more successful because I have more hair, but these other two old coots can't seem to get on board with that. It's because they're jealous."

"I don't know why they would be. Hair doesn't really make a difference. It doesn't make a difference in the character of a person anyway," she said, not meaning to slap Junior down, necessarily, just stating her opinion on the matter.

"You can say what you want. I say my hair stuck around because I made sure that it knew that I appreciated it every day, and I didn't try to scare it off by doing stupid stuff."

"Hey. I didn't do anything in my life more stupid than you have." Marshall seemed affronted.

"I didn't either. In fact, if we want to talk about stupid things, I could talk about the time that you—"

"Gentlemen," Darby interrupted. She didn't want to hear about all the exploits of the men and what they used to do.

Actually, she wouldn't mind hearing. She just wasn't sure they would be appropriate stories for Amber, and it was her job as a mother to make sure that Amber was protected.

When she got older, she could understand that sometimes men were a little more gross than a person wanted to believe.

That was a lesson for another time.

"Are you familiar with the platform, TikTok?" Marshall asked, assuming a scholarly tone to his voice.

"No. I have the app on my phone, but I hardly ever use it."

"I see." He looked like he disapproved.

"I'll ask the important question." Blaze didn't wait for Marshall to say anything else. He looked straight at Darby and said, "Can you cook?"

Darby smiled. "I'm from Maryland. I just sold a catering business that was quite successful. I developed a lot of the recipes myself, and I made them myself as well. Of course, I had employees, but I was the one who oversaw everything."

"She's hired," Junior said immediately.

There was a cough from the side of the room, and Darby turned her head.

Jonah. No wonder she felt eyes at the back of her head. He'd been standing there the whole time.

She figured she knew what that cough was for, and she wanted to tell him it wasn't necessary.

He was just looking out for her, though she was pretty sure she was going to be fine, so she gave him a little smile before she looked back to the men.

"I need to tell you men that I've already accepted a job here in Sweet Water."

"I thought you said you were looking for work?"

"You asked me what brought me to town. And since I arrived here," she looked at her watch, "an hour ago, I've already had two job offers. This one, if that's what it is, and one from..." She looked over at Jonah with her head tilted. "What did you say the name of your ranch was? Briar Patch something?"

"Sweet Briar Ranch." He lifted a brow at her, amused, but she wasn't sure why.

She turned back to the old men. "At Sweet Briar Ranch. It's a full-time position, and I'll be living there."

"Are we allowed to film on your ranch?" Marshall looked over at Jonah.

"I'm sure you will be, although if the channel takes off, my partners and I might want a cut of the video profits."

Darby managed to choke back a laugh.

It was obvious to her that he was joking, but the older men look concerned.

"Now hold on here a second, sonny. That's not right. If we do all the work, and you take a cut of our profits..."

"That's the deal I'm cutting. Take it or leave it."

"What percentage?" Marshall asked.

"I'd have to talk to my buddies, but I think a tenth of a percent would be fair."

"A tenth of a percent?" Junior said, scratching his head. "Did you mean a tenth of a percent?"

"That's what I said."

"You're just messing with us," Junior said, rolling his eyes.

"I had you there for a minute," Jonah said.

Darby smiled and shook her head. Jonah didn't seem like the kind of man who would have a huge sense of humor, and when he did, he seemed to keep a straight face as he joked.

Interesting.

It was a little hard to tell whether he was serious or not.

She liked that he wasn't a total goof-off but that he didn't have a problem laughing and having fun.

"Well, guys, she's pretty much perfect. In fact, I can't really think of anything that she's not perfect about. We can drive out to the ranch, shoot videos for an hour or two, and she can work, and we can go...what do the girls call it?"

"Edit. We can edit the videos."

"We edit the videos. We'll put one up every day."

"I can provide the music if there's a piano on the ranch," Amber said.

Every eye turned to her.

Darby wanted to grab a hold of her. She hadn't wanted that to get out. Not yet.

She tried to keep her reaction in check and not bring more attention to Amber by overreacting.

When Amber looked at her, questions in her eyes, she tried to smile reassuringly and not with the alarm that had bounced through her.

That was the reason they were there. She had left Baltimore and come West, left the ocean and everything that was familiar to her, to try to protect her daughter.

Still, she couldn't take it back, and she would never ask Amber to hide the fact that she was good at it.

"We don't have a piano, but I think that's definitely something we could make room for if it's something that you're interested in."

"Oh, I'm interested. Everyone says I'm a prodigy."

It sounded like bragging, but unfortunately, Darby winced, because it wasn't.

Chapter 6

"That was different," Jonah said, after they'd gone down the stairs and exited the building and were on their way back to Darby's car.

"I can't disagree with you there." She laughed. "I'm not even entirely sure I got the job."

"You got the job. I'm sure of it. Mostly because of Gideon and the fact that the men were completely over trying to interview all the crazy people out there. I'm sure there were sane people in amongst the crazy ones, but they got overshadowed."

"You saw some?"

"Yeah. I mean, if you think about it, it does take a certain type of person to see a video on TikTok, see the address, and drive or fly across states and possibly an entire continent on the off chance that they'll include you in their future videos."

"I see what you're saying. Not terrible people, just very adventurous ones."

"Adventurous wasn't exactly the word I was thinking of, but it works."

They got to her car, and he opened the door for Amber, remembering the side he'd seen her get out of.

He'd watched them for a while from his place inside the diner before he got out to help. It hadn't taken long to see that Darby was terrified of Billy.

"My lady," he said, making a grand gesture for Amber to get in the car.

Amber giggled and said, "Thank you, sir," and she gave a quick curtsy, even though she was wearing jeans, and scrambled in.

"You're a charmer," Darby said with humorous grin.

"I've never been accused of being a charmer before," he said. He wasn't sure what it was about these two that brought that part of him out.

He opened her door. "My lady," he said, but this was a little more mocking. He didn't want her to know that his feelings were all scrambled when it came to her. He didn't know whether to try to keep her at arm's reach or try to reach for more with her. She seemed like the kind of woman he definitely wanted to be around as much as he could, but he also had sworn that he would never marry again.

Marriage had been an abysmal failure, and while he felt most of the blame could be laid at Nora's feet, he supposed there were deficiencies in his personality.

Not to mention, he apparently stunk at picking out women to marry.

He was zero for one. And he wouldn't want to bet on the odds of him improving at all.

Plus, divorce was hard, and he didn't want to go through it again.

"If you follow me, I'll lead you to the ranch."

"All right. I... I know I said I'd take the job, but I didn't say I was going to live there."

It seemed like she felt that she needed to remind him, and he nodded.

"I understand you want to scope it out first. I also understand that sharing a bedroom with your daughter is not ideal. We have two beds in it. It used to be Elias's before he married Jane. They exchanged the bed that Jane had in her apartment for herself with the larger one that Elias had in his room. Then we added one. Not sure why, but I guess God knew."

"I see."

"But anyway, no one's going to force you to stay. And if you'd prefer to check it out and then go around town and get some advice from people, to see if we're the kind of men you can trust, you're welcome to do that. We haven't been in town long, but I think our reputation is good."

"I think that would be smart. Considering that my daughter's life is at stake."

"All right. I'll give you some names once I take you out and show you around."

"All right," she said, and from the look on her face, he got the feeling that she couldn't quite believe she was actually driving out to his ranch and had gotten a job so easily.

The job market was tight, and they had not advertised but had assumed they were not going to fill the spot easily. He knew his buddies had been praying the same as he had. He didn't know why it was always a shock when God answered a prayer so quickly and easily.

He didn't drive too fast on his way out, not knowing what kind of driver she was, and he didn't want to lose her, even though the roads were straight.

That was a nice thing about North Dakota. No one had to worry about getting carsick as they drove around the state.

They might have to worry about getting blown off the road, but that was another matter.

Today, even though it was spring, the wind wasn't too strong, just a brisk breeze going, and he hardly noticed it as he drove, hoping that he would present the house and job in such a way that she would want to stay.

Of course, whatever happened, he knew that the Lord would have a hand in it. Sometimes, he got so wrapped up in trying to make things happen the way he wanted them to, he forgot that it wasn't really supposed to be about him.

He supposed that was human nature and part of the reason God suggested, over and over, that a person spend time in God's word. Just to keep themselves grounded and to make sure that they were doing what they were supposed to do.

The ranch wasn't far out of town, and he pulled in, trying to see it from her eyes.

They'd put a pole building up last fall. It was their airplane hangar, which doubled as a garage.

They'd managed to secure a helicopter, just a small one, but it was still a score.

They needed it, since they'd gotten work for it before they even had the machine on the property.

He couldn't believe how their business had taken off, but maybe it was because their prices were low. They hadn't wanted to over-charge, and they wanted to make sure that if people were taking a chance on them, they weren't afraid of the price tag.

Still, they were set to make a hefty profit if things went the way they hoped they would.

Of course, in business, one never knew. There were all kinds of things that could happen, and he wasn't so naïve as to think that they weren't going to happen to them.

He expected there to be ups and downs. He and Gideon, and Elias to some extent, had talked about it.

Elias still owned part of the ranch, but he wasn't as invested in the crop-dusting services.

He supposed he should tell Darby that they still had two buddies, Zeke and Baker, who might be coming out. But things needed to work out in order for that to happen.

Jonah hoped things did, since they'd gotten work last fall with the idea in mind that they would all be working.

Smith, their other crew member who lived in Sweet Water and owned a part of the ranch, had already married and was helping his wife with her business.

Everything was working out, or at least most things. He hadn't expected his buddies to get married.

When Jonah had signed up for this, he figured they were all bachelors and would be batching it in North Dakota, running their businesses, and not getting involved with women.

But Smith and Elias had succumbed to the female charms right away, and Jonah had been holding his breath, expecting Gideon to do the same.

His broken leg over the winter had kept him from venturing off the ranch much, but Jonah figured it was just a matter of time.

Gideon had gone from being an outright flirt to more of a charmer, and Jonah figured he'd be finding a woman in the not-too-distant future.

He had thought that he would end up living alone on the ranch. That certainly hadn't been his thought when he'd decided to come out, but it kind of looked like that might end up being his lot.

Except, Darby would be there now. She wouldn't be his girl or anything, but she'd be in the house with him.

Along with Amber, who would lend life and, apparently, music.

He wanted to talk more about that, but Darby's expression had seemed to indicate that it was something that she didn't want to share.

Jonah hadn't been able to figure out why, but he figured later he would just ask her.

They pulled up to the house, white and weather-beaten, a two-story with a bunch of bedrooms and hardwood floors. Drafty, and misshapen, as it had been added onto in sections over the years.

If Darby stayed, they'd probably be putting on an addition again, which Gideon would be able to handle, since that was his thing.

Except Gideon had a commitment to put an addition on for a woman outside of Sweet Water. He hadn't been able to do it because of his broken leg, but Jonah wouldn't want him to do anything else until he'd fulfilled that obligation.

Still, there were no flowers in the flower beds, just last year's weeds beaten down with snow. The walk was a little overrun, and the porch was empty with nothing but a couple of rocking chairs and a swing on it.

None of the knickknacks that women seemed to like.

He hadn't even considered that. Normally he didn't think that way, but he was trying to think about it the way Darby would.

Would she want to stay here?

He got out of his pickup and waited for her car to stop before he walked around and opened the door, letting Amber out first, who grinned at him, liking the VIP treatment.

By the time Amber had crawled out, Darby already had her door open and was standing up.

"It's pretty isolated here," she said.

He didn't think that boded well, that that was the first comment she could think of saying.

He couldn't refute it, either. She was right. There was no point in him trying to pretend she wasn't.

"Our closest neighbors are a mile and a half away, and that's if you go through the fields."

"I didn't see any animals."

"We have a couple steers behind the barn. We had thought about getting chicks, but with our schedules being so erratic, we weren't sure whether there'd be anyone around to feed them or not. We weren't entirely sure who we'd be getting to take care of the place, and whether or not we had chicks would be up to them."

"We could have chicks?" Amber asked, her eyes big, looking at her mom like that was the best thing that could ever happen to her.

"If we stay here, we'd be here every day and we could feed them."

"We'd provide the feed and all the equipment. They need a waterer, a feeder, and a place to stay at night that will keep them safe from predators. But, yeah. It'd be your job to take care of them."

"We'd have our own eggs! I could gather eggs?"

"I would say so," Darby said, and Jonah understood why Amber had said she was a pushover.

It was obvious that she wanted her daughter to have every good thing, or maybe she just wanted to make up for something. He wasn't sure what.

"Come on in. I'll show you the office. It's not much to speak of, and then I'll take you upstairs. Show you around before we talk business."

"Maybe, if it's okay, Amber can play outside?" Darby asked, and Jonah had a sinking feeling in his stomach.

He wasn't sure why. With the way he'd been feeling since he'd met Darby, he would have thought he'd be ecstatic to have the potential of being alone with her, but he wasn't. He was...nervous. Or apprehensive.

He shoved those feelings aside and tried to make his voice sound normal.

"She sure can. There's nothing that could hurt her, and we can hardly lose her. In fact, if you want, once I show you the office and everything, we can talk out on the porch."

"I guess that would make me feel better. She's only eight, and while she doesn't need to have us looking at her every second, this is a new area for her, and I just like to keep an eye on her."

"Mom. I'll be fine. You know I'm always fine," Amber said, in a pleading voice.

"Of course you will be. And you can play. I'll just be watching you. Let's go see our room first. And see the room where I'll be working while we stay here."

Jonah went in, turning right and going up the stairs to the bed-rooms. "All of these others are taken, so you'll have this one. There is one down at the end of the hall. It's not ready to have people staying in it, so if you decide to stay, we could probably get it ready. But we also have buddies who are potentially coming out, and they'll need a place to stay. If they come, that room will have to be for them."

He hadn't wanted to admit that. Had wanted her to think that she would be able to have a room to herself and have her daughter have a room to herself, too, but he didn't want to deceive her. Or to give her false hope about something.

"That's fine. I think the most important thing right now is a strong lock on the door. I want to feel safe."

"I should have grabbed one at the hardware store before we came out. But I can do that after we're done talking. I'll have it on for you if you decide to stay tonight."

"I don't want to push you for it."

"I don't want you to not feel safe. That's the only thing that you've told me so far that you really want to have, so I'll make sure it gets done. It's not going to be a hardship."

And he meant that. She had not asked for anything. Just seemed grateful for what was happening and willing to do whatever needed to be done. The very least he could do would be to make sure she got the one thing she'd mentioned twice now.

"There's two bedrooms down the hall. One room, the room I'm staying in right now, has a bathroom attached to it. All the other ones share that bathroom there. I could probably get Gideon to share with me so that it's just you and your daughter. But if Zeke and Baker end up coming, you're going to have to share. I'm sorry."

He wished he could change that. Wished he didn't have to tell her that. But again, he had to be honest. He didn't want to sugarcoat things and have her take a job only to find out later that things weren't the way he'd said they'd be.

It wouldn't be honest of him, she would be annoyed, and he would look like a liar. And rightfully so.

"All right. That sounds fair."

"There's a tub and a shower, the usual stuff in the bathroom. We keep a hamper in there, and right now, we guys are taking turns washing the towels, but we all wash our own clothes." He hesitated, not wanting to overwhelm her but knowing what they'd talked about and not wanting her to be surprised. "We were hoping that the person we hired would do laundry and some cooking as well."

"Yes. You mentioned that. And I don't see why I can't. As long as the bookwork is something that I'm able to do and doesn't take up all my time."

"I don't think it's going to be exceptionally difficult. If you're used to using scheduling software, this will probably be intuitive for you," he said as he walked out of the bedroom that he'd just shown her and followed her back down the stairs.

He continued, "It's just a matter of invoicing, and receiving payments, going to the bank, that type of thing. It shouldn't be an excessive amount of things. Just...things that need to be done."

"All right. Sounds like everything I've done before. When you own your own business, that's just the way it goes. Unless you hire someone," she said, with a little bit of humor in her voice, since that's exactly what he was doing.

"You're right there. There was a lot more red tape than what I had anticipated. Thankfully, we were planning on starting in the spring, or we might have run into a jam."

He figured the office was the next most important thing, so he led her to a room that was slightly off the main part of the house.

"This doesn't have its own outside entrance, but we've talked about putting one in. I don't think the guys will be here much, and we won't need to go in and out a lot. So, if you live here, it's not a big deal. The main reason we were thinking of adding one was if the person we hired didn't stay here."

"Oh, I see. Either way, it doesn't matter to me."

She didn't look dismayed at the state of the office. It was just a bare desk with a laptop sitting on it. There wasn't even a phone on the desk.

"We all use our cell phones. We probably won't have a telephone. But we do have a printer. It's over there." He pointed to the corner, where the printer sat on the floor. "We actually had to redo this room. It wasn't finished inside, so we wired it up, got the drywall finished and painted, but we haven't put the counters in yet. Hoping to do that this coming week."

"And then the printer won't be on the floor anymore."

"Exactly."

"Can I have a desk in here?" Amber asked. She smiled at Jonah, and Jonah understood how it was so hard for Darby to tell her no.

Darby looked surprised, then a little embarrassed that her child would be so forward.

Before Darby could correct her, he found himself saying, "I think that's a good idea. We'll have to make sure you get one."

Amber beamed, and Darby smiled.

He figured those were probably the right words. And he also figured if Amber came to live with his buddies and him, she would be spoiled beyond words.

Maybe it would be a good thing they wouldn't be there much. He couldn't imagine Gideon or Baker or Zeke being able to tell her no any more than he could.

"All right. So that's the office. That's probably where we'll keep all of the things that have to do with the business. Sometimes we work around the kitchen table, because a lot of times, we're talking business as we eat supper and into the evening. But this is where we'll try to keep everything. Oh. We're getting filing cabinets too. Even though most stuff will probably be electronic."

"All right. Sounds good."

She seemed like she was doing okay with everything that he had shown her so far. As he led her around the downstairs, she seemed okay with the kitchen too, which was a typical big farmhouse kitchen with a couple of windows, cupboards, and countertops around the periphery with a wooden butcher block table in the middle.

It was big enough to seat six comfortably and eight in a pinch.

She seemed impressed with the amount of counterspace, and she definitely loved the kitchen table, running her hand over it and murmuring, "Extraordinary. I've seen these in pictures but never actually touched one, let alone thought I'd eat at one. I love it."

He hadn't really thought it was that great, but then again, it was just a piece of furniture that he used to meet his needs. Not something he sat around admiring. He had a feeling he and Darby were different in that regard.

"Can I go play now?" Amber asked, the second it seemed like they might be finished with perusing the kitchen.

"You sure can," Darby said. "If that's okay?" She raised her brows and looked at him.

He nodded, catching her eyes again. There was just something compelling about her. He hadn't lost the urge to make everything look as good as he could so that she'd not just take the job but live with them. He wanted her here.

Very odd feelings, especially for him. Normally he was very realistic and didn't get swept away by the things that he felt.

That had all changed with Darby. He wasn't sure he liked it.

"I can grab us a drink if you want to sit down on the porch?"

"I don't need anything. The chicken was so good, and I'm still full from that."

"All right." He led her through the dining room and out the front door onto the front porch.

Amber moseyed down the steps, not running off like he would have at her age.

Maybe it was the difference between boys and girls, or maybe it was something to do with Amber. He wasn't sure. Whatever it was, he watched her go, thinking what a cute little girl she was.

Of course, he thought her mother was pretty wonderful as well. Maybe he shouldn't be pushing for her to take the job. Maybe he should be pushing for her not to. Maybe he shouldn't have offered it in the first place. Since she had such a strange hold on him.

Whatever it was, he didn't seem to be able to resist her, and he knew he was going to do everything in his power to make their conversation go the way he wanted it to.

Chapter 7

D arby had been impressed with the house. Their room was big, even though it had two beds, but there was no private bathroom.

She didn't like the idea of her daughter and her sharing a bathroom with men she barely knew, but they seemed like nice men, and if what Jonah said was true, they wouldn't be there much anyway.

Next winter might be different, but by then, she'd have a good idea of what to expect. At least she thought so.

And she couldn't have found a more ideal situation for Amber, if Jonah wanted to be a dad.

But she couldn't take this job without letting him know first., After all, if she took the job and he found out and wasn't interested in being a dad, it would be awkward all around if she stayed.

She sat down on the swing, and after a moment, he walked over and sat on one of the rocking chairs facing her, across the porch from her. It was only six or seven feet between them, but it felt too far and not far enough.

She wasn't used to such conflicting emotions, and she tried to get a hold of herself. She needed to just be honest and tell him the truth.

The cards would fall where they would, and she would do what she needed to do in order to protect her child.

"So Amber plays the piano?" he asked, seeming to think that this was a natural way to begin their conversation.

Or maybe he'd picked up on her discomfort when Amber had mentioned it before.

Amber was out of earshot, walking through the yard, examining a couple of piles of lumber and a wheelbarrow, along with an old shed and what might have been a chicken coop.

She wasn't used to any of those things, since they hadn't had anything like that in their townhouse in Baltimore.

"She does."

Maybe this would be a good lead into the conversation she needed to have.

Lord, please help me say the right things. Please don't let the emotions I'm feeling get all muddled up and make me say things I shouldn't or make me try to turn the conversation in the way I want it to go personally. I want what's best for Amber.

"I have to admit that I have some things I need to tell you."

"All right," he said, a note of caution in his tone, but he still sounded casual and relaxed.

So far, so good.

"I'm not sure where to start. So forgive me if I stumble."

"There's no pressure. I'm not sure what your information is, but I'm not worried about it. You seem like a person who has integrity and character, and I'm not going to judge you."

"That's good to know, but I suppose that's not exactly the direction I was going to go."

"All right. I'll shut up and you can talk."

She smiled as he leaned back in the rocking chair, threading his fingers together and laying them over top of his chest. A pose that said *I'm patiently waiting, and I'm listening.*

She couldn't meet his eyes. They were too compelling, so she looked out over the yard.

"Amber is a piano prodigy. She has been able to play the piano since she first touched one at three years old. She has gotten better over the years, but...this is where I'm going to cut off and start at the beginning." She wasn't sure what else to do, and the beginning seemed like the best place.

"All right. Go ahead." His voice was easy. He didn't seem overly surprised or interested in Amber's ability.

"When I was a senior in college, I volunteered at a pregnancy center. Not an abortion clinic. It was a center where women could go if they found themselves unexpectedly pregnant and didn't want to have an abortion. Or wanted to know what other choices they had."

"That's a good thing." His words seemed cautious, like he was wondering when she was going to get to the part that was going to be hard.

Oh, if he only knew. It was coming. It was definitely coming.

"I met a woman there who was pregnant. She had just gotten out of a marriage. It had not been a good marriage, according to her. And she at first thought she wouldn't keep the child, but as she continued with her pregnancy, she decided that she would have the baby, but she wanted to give it up for adoption immediately."

Darby looked down at her hands, gently pushing the swing enough to make it sway. "She told me the father wasn't interested. That he was in the military, he moved around, he hadn't been available in their marriage, hadn't been interested in her. He spent all his time with his friends. The kind of thing that you know there's probably another side to the story, but that was her side."

"I see," he said.

She thought maybe he did. And she had wanted to be fair. Had wanted to give him her side of the story but let him know she knew there was another side.

"So, anyway, this woman and I became friends. If you could call it that. I worked there, and we didn't see each other apart from the crisis center, which also had apartments that were for rent for low-income mothers. Places where they could go if they needed a place to stay. We handed out clothes, baby bags, formula, pretty much anything they needed or wanted, and we even offered free babysitting to a point."

"Wow. Nice place."

"It was. It was definitely a place that I wish there were more of in the country. That wasn't what my major was, or anything, but it just really felt like I was doing a good thing. And this woman and I really clicked." She swallowed. "There...came a point where she asked me to adopt her baby."

"Wow."

"Yes. I was honored. And floored. But she also had been thinking about getting an abortion, so it wasn't like she was giving me something that was extremely valuable to her. She just thought that I would do a good job of raising her child. And she liked the idea of me getting her versus the couples she had met. She didn't think too highly of any of them and told me that she was sure I could do a better job alone than they could with two parents."

"That's a compliment."

"I guess. I wasn't sure about that, and I always felt that it took a mom and a dad to raise a baby, but I kind of got invested with this woman and her baby. I already loved her even though she wasn't born. I went with her to all of her doctors' appointments. I heard the heartbeat, saw ultrasounds, and she even asked me to be in the labor and delivery room when she delivered."

"I'm assuming this baby was Amber?"

"Yes. I adopted Amber when she was born. There is no father's name on the birth certificate. Amber...doesn't know. I... I never told her I adopted her. I suppose I should have. But I thought it was going to be hard enough being a single mom. I didn't want to have to answer adoption questions."

He looked like he wasn't sure he agreed with that. She had thought long and hard about it, and, if she had to do it again, she supposed a child had a right to know that they were adopted. It will be a devastating thing when Amber found out that she wasn't her biological mother. She lived in dread of that day

Hopefully, whatever he thought, he realized that Darby had done her very best.

"So, I took Amber home when she was discharged from the hospital. This woman kept in contact with me. She ended up remarrying, and getting a job, then going through another divorce. I stayed with her through it all. One day, she was at my house visiting, and she heard Amber, who was five at the time, playing piano."

"Oh." That was all he said, but the word held so much. She thought he understood.

"Yeah. She started to get on me, about was I making sure Amber got lessons and was I taking her to all the places that she should be taken to for a child who had that kind of talent, and was I having her audition for TV shows and for talent contests and for various things, and... I just didn't feel like that was something I wanted my child to do."

"I don't blame you. There is a lot of danger in those kinds of things."

"I know. There are a lot of good things too. I didn't want to keep anything good from her. I didn't want to close any doors. I didn't want to not give her the opportunities that her talent would offer her," Darby said, and she could hear the pleading in her voice, wanting him to understand. "But I didn't want it to be a moneymaking thing. I didn't want it to be a freak show. A business where we were more concerned about making money than we were concerned about letting a little girl grow up. I...wish I had someone to help me, but I just prayed about it and was doing the best I could."

She looked down at her lap, her fingers picking at a seam on her jeans.

"She had piano lessons and teachers, and she had a very limited number of places where she played. She was only five at the time."

"That's a lot of responsibility for a five-year-old, to play in front of people."

"True. But Amber loved it. Piano is her instrument, and she loves playing. You can see the expression on her face when she plays, she's just transported somewhere beautiful, and it makes me so happy to see her. I could never, ever take that away from her."

"I don't think I would have thought that."

"No. I didn't. That's just what her birth mother started accusing me of. Of being selfish, stifling her, not letting her live up to her full potential. She... She had gotten divorced and needed a place to stay. She wanted to stay with me, and... I turned her down."

"Ouch."

"Yeah. Every time I met her, she was on me about making sure that Amber got taken here and there and everywhere. And I just couldn't live with that kind of pressure. I was trying to run the business, and I was trying to make sure that Amber had a normal childhood. As normal as possible. With some special things thrown in, but not so special that they were everything to her." She sighed. "I don't know if I found a good balance or not, but I didn't want her to be a freak that couldn't get along in society, like children often are if they've been taken away from everything, forced to practice six or eight hours a day."

"That's excessive."

"The thing is, I think Amber would love it. She would love to play the piano that many hours a day. But for her, playing the piano is like another child playing regular childhood games. Children might love to play six or eight hours all day every day, but it's not going to help them grow up into a healthy adult if they do that."

"No. Of course not." His hands moved on his chest. "If you're try-ing to say that it's important that Amber has time to play the piano, I told you that we'll make sure we get one. You saw the house. It's not like it's crowded with furniture and we'd have trouble finding a spot for it. We'll make room. And if it's something important, we'll make it a priority. No one's going to care if she plays the piano at any hour. Gideon sleeps like a log, the second he lies down, he's snoring. I have slightly more restraint, but I can sleep through anything as well."

"I hadn't even considered that, but it's good to know." She bit her lip. That wasn't what she was trying to get at, and now she had kind of lost her train of thought. And she wasn't sure what to say.

"Was there something else bothering you?" he asked after a moment, like he could see her agitation and wanted her to know he was still listening.

"Yeah. Not bothering me, just...something I need to say." She looked across the yard, where Amber was opening the door to what looked like an old chicken coop.

"I'll wait as long as you need. Take your time."

Some people would say that sarcastically, but Jonah seemed like he meant it. He leaned back in the rocking chair, looking as relaxed as he had the entire time.

"All right. I left Baltimore because I wanted to protect Amber. Her mother had been getting more insistent, and she had gone to the authorities several times. She is the birth mother, although her name is not on the birth certificate, and I have all rights. Still, she was trying to get the adoption records unsealed and was trying to make things difficult for me."

"Basically she was looking at Amber and seeing dollar signs?"

"I hate to say that. She's her mom. She gave birth to her anyway. But...she claimed to want what was in Amber's best interests. And maybe, maybe I am sheltering her too much. Not letting her use her talent like she could, but...it just felt like her mom wanted to push her, to drive her to be more, and... Yeah. There was money involved, and that can make things ugly. Just because, with her trying to get the records unsealed, I felt like maybe she was trying to take my child."

She said that last part kind of quickly. That was her biggest fear. Amber being stolen from her and being treated like a money-making machine, instead of a child. Yes, a child with a great and amazing ability, but still a child.

"Well, other than not telling her that she was adopted, and I don't really know about that. I don't know what to say, but otherwise... I agree with you. She should have a childhood and not be forced, or even allowed, to only have one thing she's good at, playing piano."

"That's right. I mean she's in a normal school, with normal kids, and she just takes piano lessons on the side. Now, granted, she's really good at them, and occasionally she has a weekend where we have to go somewhere and play. But it's not every weekend. It's not all the time, and I don't allow her to practice for more than an hour a day."

"Wow. You have to limit her practicing time?"

"Yeah. But there's one more wrinkle in all of this."

"Okay." He seemed a lot more guarded now, now that more of the story had come out. He seemed to know that it wasn't just an ordinary, run-of-the-mill situation. That there might be something else going on.

Not dangerous, just something that was going to shift his whole world. She was almost certain he could sense it.

Chapter 8

"I told you that the mother told me that the father wasn't interested in the baby. That was what she said when she was pregnant." Darby bit her lip. "But late one night, we were talking about Amber, and she was telling me about the potential for her making money and listing all of the ways she could earn it, and something she said made me ask about the dad. If he knew, shouldn't we be talking to him about it? I don't remember what made me ask that, because he had been a nonissue in either of our lives."

"All right."

"She mentioned his name to me for the first time, and then she dropped a bombshell. She said he didn't even know about the baby."

"Oh."

She let that hang there for a minute, not because she wanted to include any kind of dramatic effect, but because she wasn't sure what direction to go. She hadn't dropped the biggest shock yet; she'd been skirting around it, afraid.

"The woman's name, the birth mother of Amber, her name was Nora."

She held her breath. If he was the Jonah Mills that Nora had mentioned, which she was fairly certain he was, since he had a history in the Air Force, and when she casually asked Nora for a little bit more info, she had searched for him on the internet and was able to piece things together through the business he and his friends had started.

If they hadn't had that online presence, she might not have figured it out.

Still, she waited.

"Nora?" he said, and his voice sounded ominous.

"Yes."

"Nora... What last name was she using?"

"When I knew her, it was Reynolds. Then she got married and changed it, then she changed it back to Nora Reynolds after the divorce. But she said the father was Jonah Mills."

"How old is Amber?"

"She's eight. She was born in September."

He was processing, and she didn't say anything, but she did pull out her phone. She stood up, pulling up her photo app and getting the picture that she had saved earlier.

She turned the phone around so he could see it. "This is Nora."

"Holy smokes," Jonah breathed.

That's all he said while he stared at the picture.

"That's my ex-wife." He looked around. "I don't have any pictures of her, but that's my ex-wife."

"You don't need to prove it. I did some digging and was fairly sure that I had found the correct Jonah Mills. He lived in Sweet Water. You matched everything I knew about him."

"You weren't here looking for a job! You were here to find me. To ambush me." There was accusation in his tone as he looked at her with reproachful eyes.

She had been afraid he was going to be angry at her. Kill the messenger or whatever. Or just because he found fault with the way she handled things. She hadn't been perfect. She could see it easily looking back. At the very least, she should have told Amber she was adopted from the beginning. That truth haunted her days.

But she had tried. And she would keep trying.

In her defense, she said, "I am looking for a job. Did you not hear me? I sold my business and left Baltimore because she was trying to turn Amber into some kind of moneymaking machine, steal her childhood, and take my rights as her mother. When she dropped your name, I did what any sane person would do and looked you up. Because, by that time, I knew Nora was a compulsive liar, and when she mentioned that the father didn't know he had a daughter, I knew, even though I had adopted her legally and completely, that I would never keep that kind of information from a man who wanted to have a relationship with his daughter. I couldn't."

Her words came out soft, but she allowed her own anger to show, that he would have the audacity to not believe her. She wasn't the bad guy in this. She was trying to do the right thing. She just...

"I didn't know how to approach you. How do you walk up to some man and say, 'by the way, you have a daughter you don't know about?'"

She looked at him. The anger drained out of him. He stared at her.

"I didn't know how to do it. I might not have done it the very best way. Honest to God, I tried. I ran the circumstances over in my head, trying to figure it out." She looked away, dropping her phone back in her pocket and taking a deep breath. "I had no idea the first person I would meet in Sweet Water, North Dakota, would be the man I was looking for. What are the odds?"

"They're pretty good."

She huffed out a breath. "I...I had a name, Charlene something, that I had been given when I had tried to look for information regarding Sweet Water."

"I know her. I can take you to her when we're done here."

He was obviously reeling. He had stood and probably didn't even notice that his arm touched her shoulder as he stood, hands at his side like he was ready to grab a hold of something, watching the little girl in the yard.

"I thought she looked familiar. It never even occurred to me that she looked like Nora. Man. I'm so dumb sometimes."

"Maybe she looks like you. She has your eyes."

"She does?" He looked at her, a half grin on his face.

"Yeah. I noticed that right off, as soon as I could see them under your cowboy hat. They are the same warm brown that Amber has."

"Amber. My daughter. That's crazy. I can't even believe it."

"I know it's going to take some adjusting and getting used to."

"Does she know?"

"My goodness, no!" Darby said immediately and fast. "I couldn't tell her. I didn't know what you would be like, or what your reaction would be, or if you'd even want her. I was not going to get her hopes up that we were going to go meet her dad or something, only to have you not be interested."

"I'm interested. Man, I'm extremely interested."

He shoved a hand through his hair, settling his hat back on his head, and then he turned, walking around her, pacing to the other side of the porch before he came back.

"I'm a father."

"Sorry. I know it was a shock. That's why it took me so long to tell you, I...wasn't relishing the idea, although I hoped it would be good news."

"It's good news. Again, mostly. I'm surprised, and amazed, and angry at Nora for not telling me. Because she did not tell me, I swear it. I had no idea she was pregnant. She walked out, and I was relieved, but I wouldn't have allowed her to just give our baby away, if I could have had any say in it."

"Well, it's a blessing that the crisis pregnancy center was there, because Amber almost wasn't born."

He had no idea how true that statement was. She had spent many nights talking through the night with Nora, trying to convince her that having her baby was the best thing for both of them. That she wouldn't have to live with the regret of an abortion. With the idea that she had killed her own child for the rest of her life, that she wouldn't have those emotional scars, that the baggage would be gone. During one of those conversations, Nora had asked her to be Amber's mom.

"Maybe I have you to thank for that."

"Maybe. I know I talked to her a lot about it. But a lot of people deserve credit, because if people hadn't had the vision for the crisis pregnancy center, if people hadn't built it, hadn't donated money, staffed it..."

"I know. I know. But Nora is not exactly known as a selfless kind of person. She would have taken the easy way out if she possibly could have. I know that, and someone had to walk her around, helping her see the best way." He closed his mouth, almost deliberately, like he didn't want to say anything more about her.

"I know what you're talking about. You don't have to say anything more. I think we're all like that. She was against the wall and didn't know if she could look after herself and her baby too."

"I didn't want her to go," he ground out, looking at Darby, like it was important that she believed him.

"I believe you. I think that's why I said before that there were two sides to every story. She told her side, making herself look as good as she could. It's... It's uncommon to find someone who will try to tell the truth, even when it puts them in a bad light."

"I know. At the time, I would have blamed everything on her, just as it looks like she blamed everything on me. But over the years, I've seen how I could have been better. Could have done more, could have been a husband who loved and cherished my wife, instead of expecting her to just deal. I wasn't as good as I could have been, and I was selfish too."

"Don't beat yourself up over it. We all are."

"But my daughter could have had a father all this time if I had been better."

"True, you could have had the last eight years with your daughter, but I promise you, I've done my very best with her. And now, I want her to know you." She took a breath. "And I was hoping that together, we can fight off whatever it is that Nora wants to do. It might even turn out to be nothing. Once I'm not around anymore, she might just give up. In fact, I'm kind of hoping that will be it. She's not exactly known as someone who sticks with things."

"Tell me about it," he said, with irony in his voice.

Darby didn't even take the time to smile, because she wanted him to be on board with her. She wanted his verbal agreement. Just that he acknowledged that he was on her side. Or whatever. She wasn't even sure.

"You'll help me?" she finally just said. Simple. A plea.

"Of course." He spoke immediately, like there was no doubt. "I don't want to fight anybody, but if you adopted her, she's yours. Nora is not going to undo that or take her back, now that she thinks she might have some kind of value. That's just so...wrong."

"Yeah. And I've tried to shelter Amber from all of this, so I don't think she has any idea. She knows Nora, and Nora didn't seem to be super interested in her when she was younger. Not until she turned five and she saw her play."

"You spent three years dealing with this?"

"I thought she would go away. Like I said, she's not known as someone who sticks with things. And I had a business. It's not easy to just walk away from it. I had to find someone who would buy it. That took time. I decided last year this time I was going to sell, and that's how long it took to get things straightened out."

"Wow. And Nora harassed you the whole time?"

"She would come and go. I would see her for a while, and then it was like she would get distracted by something else, then she'd come back, so I was just kind of hoping that if I could move away, she'd stop."

She looked out over the yard where Amber knelt down, her hand stretched out toward a cat who looked at her cautiously.

"I really don't think Nora has a leg to stand on. I'm not a hundred percent certain, but I have a lawyer on it, and he assured me that she had given up her rights, totally signed them away, and I have been a completely competent mom. I have witnesses. People who will back me up. There's no way, according to my lawyer, that she can take her. But I didn't want her to poison Amber."

"Yeah."

"I heard her telling Amber how big and famous she could be if she played the piano in front of lots of people. She was painting such a beautiful picture. She didn't talk about the travel schedule, and all the hard work, and the fact that she wouldn't be able to go to school and play with her friends, and that she would be different from everyone else, different in a good way, because everybody's different, but different also in the way that she wouldn't have the normal experiences that a child had. I just want her to have a childhood, and then maybe when she's a little older, or gradually, she can get into it if she wants to. I just... I want to do it right. Not look at dollar signs and go rushing in because I see money."

"It sounds to me like your way is the best way," he said immediately, and she tried hard not to breathe an audible sigh of relief. She hadn't expected him to jump on that bandwagon and want the money, and she'd been pretty sure he wasn't that type, but she hadn't known for sure what he was going to say until he said it.

She wouldn't admit that, though.

Then, she thought, why not?

Chapter 9

“Thank you. That’s what I needed to hear. I was concerned that you might be after the money too.” Darby knew she had taken a big risk in telling him everything.

Her lawyer said that since he hadn’t known about the adoption and hadn’t signed off on it, there was a possibility that he could get a DNA test, prove that he was the father, and then try to take his parental rights.

She wouldn’t have said anything if she had had doubts. But at the same time, she knew she couldn’t work for him, with his daughter right under his nose, and not tell him.

“I had to take the risk that you might not be on board with me, and tell you. Just because I felt like it wasn’t the right thing to do, to hold back from you. My hope is that we can decide together what’s best for Amber, and even though I have custody, I…hope that I’ll be able to be an adult about this and share…time with her if that’s what you want.”

“I’m still reeling. Still processing, but it seems to me that you actually just brought about the very best situation possible.” He looked at her, with his brows raised. “You and I are actually going to be living in the same house. So, I’ll get to spend time with her, because I should be here some. I…can’t believe how it worked out.”

“It was a good thing. Honestly, I had no idea what to do when I walked into Sweet Water, I just knew I had to get here to be where you were and to meet you. After that, I had no plan. I promise.”

“That was pretty brave of you.”

"I don't know if it was bravery, but I definitely was taking a chance. But it just felt like the Lord was leading me, and as much as I didn't want to, I knew this was the right thing to do. I just didn't know how it was going to work out."

"We still don't. But... But...I think we can work together."

She smiled, feeling a weight lift off her shoulders for the first time in a really long time. "I know. We just met today, but I have that feeling too. I just feel...different with you. And don't take it wrong, because I'm not trying to say that to get brownie points or anything like that. I think we'll be like anyone else, where we have a child between us, and sometimes we're going to disagree. But there was just something about you. Something that resonated rightly with me."

She couldn't tell him about the attraction. And there was something beyond that anyway. She wouldn't just trust a man because she felt attracted to him. That was about the dumbest thing a person could ever do.

Not that she hadn't made plenty of mistakes in her life along those lines before.

"All right. This is all new to me. Can you...tell me about her?"

She smiled to herself. He was interested. He seemed like he cared. He seemed like he wanted to know. She couldn't have asked for more.

She said a silent prayer of thanks to the Lord, that there was potential here for Jonah to love Amber just as much as she did.

"Well, obviously she loves to play the piano. And by the way, she's also an expert on pianos, even at eight years old. So, if you're interested in buying a piano, she'll have lots to say about it. But she will want you to buy the most expensive piano out there. Most likely. And she'll have a list of reasons why."

"I see."

"Yeah. Anyway, about that, I have money set back. I sold the piano that we had in our townhouse in Baltimore, and that money is going toward a new piano wherever we land, I just couldn't say anything until I knew..."

"I get it."

"So, don't worry about that."

She took a breath. That was important. Amber needed a piano. Darby didn't want her talent to be exploited, but she also wanted her to have the instrument she needed to nurture her gift.

"Just hang on a second. Are there any other bombshells?" He put a hand up, as though warding her off but also as though he wanted to ward off any other bad news.

"No. As you could probably figure out from what I just said, it's not typical for an eight-year-old to know all about pianos. She's...even without being a piano prodigy, she's not an average child."

She kinda hated to say that. Like there was something odd about her, because she did well on standardized tests and talked like an adult.

"I see. So she's smart?"

"Yeah. She's really smart. When you talk to her for any length of time, it's like talking to a little adult, but even though she sounds intelligent, she still has the maturity level of an eight-year-old. So, it's easy to forget when you start talking to her that you're not really talking to an adult, because her verbal skills, and even her reasoning to some extent, is so advanced."

"I guess she got that from her mother." He laughed, although there was not a lot of humor in it, but at least he seemed to be settling around the idea that he had a daughter and didn't seem quite as shell-shocked as he had earlier in their conversation.

"I don't know. I met Nora, and she's really nice, but sometimes I wondered where Amber's intelligence came from, and I assumed it must be you."

"All right. After you know me for a while, you can let me know if you still think that," he said with a bit of a grin, and she thought he might even be joking.

He laughed, and she realized he was.

She liked that, that he wasn't letting this derail him but that he was going to roll with it.

"Do you think we can tell her that I'm her dad?"

"I think that we should. But you might want to wait until you know her a little bit? Or I don't know. It just seems like a lot to spring on her all at once. Although, if you're eager... Do it how you want to do it," she finally ended up saying. She didn't know what to do. "This is one of those things where I'm not sure what's best. You know? Like, just not sure whether we should dump it on her all at once, or let her adjust to the move, or what. I always fear making a mistake."

"I know. Sometimes in our lives, we're not sure which way to go. My tendency is to just pick a way and start out with it. But as I've gotten older, I've realized that sometimes God just wants me to stand still and wait for Him. It's like a test. Do I have the faith to wait?"

She wanted to cheer. Just shout and be excited. She couldn't believe what he was saying. That he wanted the Lord to be involved in his life and his decisions with Amber.

She had prayed that her father would be a Christian, but Nora hadn't said, and Darby hadn't wanted to put up a bunch of red flags by asking a lot of questions about him.

She'd gotten the information she needed in order to look him up, and she hadn't wanted to push for any more, just in case it would make Nora suspicious.

She hadn't wanted Nora to get in touch with Jonah before she could.

She had told the story with the facts as she saw them, trying not to sugarcoat anything to make herself look better than she was.

She hadn't always made all the right decisions, she hadn't always done everything perfectly. But she could say with assurance that her main goal had always been to do her very best and make the very best decisions possible for Amber.

If that hadn't happened, if she'd messed up, it wasn't because she hadn't tried to do the right way.

Hopefully, Jonah would see that and believe her.

"What does she like, beyond piano?"

"She didn't want to leave her friends in Baltimore, and she wants me to get her registered for school here as soon as possible. I thought I would do that tomorrow."

"Yeah. You hadn't mentioned if you want to live here for sure, but if you do, it wasn't like we needed someone to start this second."

"Good. I... I have luggage in my car, and I do want to speak to the ladies in Sweet Water, just to be extra safe, but I'm thinking that we'll stay here tonight, if you get the lock on the door, and I'll start soon, but not tomorrow."

"Sounds good. We'll have paperwork to fill out, but we can do that sometime."

"Yeah." She thought about what he'd asked about Amber. She hadn't told him much, and he seemed interested, so she shared some more. "She loves school. She loves math. Which is odd, I thought, considering that her talent is music, but there is math in music, and that seems to be the way her brain is wired."

"Maybe she's like me after all. I always loved math."

"Maybe, because I'm pretty sure Nora hated it." She didn't say anything more, but Nora hadn't seemed to like anything that had to do with school. Not math or reading or anything. "She likes spaghetti. That's her favorite meal. Although she really liked the chicken that we ate today. She likes chicken nuggets and French fries, hot dogs, and all the junk food that Americans eat but shouldn't." She smiled.

He grinned. "Guilty."

"Her favorite color is pink. She is such a girl. She likes flowing dresses, but she also has a little bit of a tomboy in her, too, and if you were serious about the chicks, I know she would love them. She is such an animal lover, but we weren't allowed pets in our townhouse."

"The guys and I have talked about getting a dog, but again, since we were going to be gone, we didn't. I want to say since you're going to be here, we could, but I don't want to get so many animals that you have three hours of work to do morning and night just taking care of them."

"No. I don't want that either. A dog is a little bit bigger commitment than chicks. Maybe... Maybe if we decide this is a long-term thing, we could do a dog?"

"Yeah. We'll talk about that. I guess we'll talk about a lot of things. And just try to always do what's best for Amber."

"Yeah."

"It's going to be a shift for me, because I'm not used to having to think about anyone but myself. Since Nora left, that's all there's been."

"I suspect that it's not going to be as hard for you as what you think." She smiled, believing her words to be true.

Chapter 10

June looked at her calendar.

It was hard to believe it had been two weeks since her last treatment.

Touching her head, which was still completely bald, she smiled a little. Soon. Soon there would be fuzzy new growth.

Losing her hair had not been the worst thing that had happened to her in her life. It was just one small bump in the road.

At least that's what she told herself. It seemed like a big thing at the time, when she'd first held big clumps of hair in her fist as the first bald spot showed the shiny pink of her head.

Funny how one little thing could make her feel feminine and beautiful, and losing it could make her feel the exact opposite.

Of course, her husband hadn't been terribly supportive.

He hadn't told her that she was beautiful when she lay on the couch, crying and sick, mourning everything that seemed to be taken from her. She wasn't beautiful and she knew it, but he could have said something to make her feel better.

Interesting, since he didn't seem to have trouble lying to her about other things. That would have been a lie, one she would have spotted immediately, one she would have hoped there was some truth behind. Truth in that he didn't need her to have hair in order to look at her and think she was beautiful on the inside, her personality, her character and integrity, her heart, her love for people.

But, there had been no such comforting, encouraging words from her husband.

She moved away from the counter to the sink, where dirty dishes from last night's supper still sat. She also needed to figure out what she was making for supper this evening.

Before she started supper, she wanted to check her online business. She made and maintained websites for several dozen customers, and to her surprise they seem to like what she had done, and she had more inquiries from potential clients than she could take on.

Who would have thought that she, June Bingley, would have a business that was successful and actually making money?

Her cell phone rang from the counter, and she reached over, swiping, seeing it was her daughter Juliann calling from college.

"Hello?" she said, smiling. It was always a good day when her children called her.

"Mom? How are you?"

"I'm fine. I finally feel like the chemo fog is starting to lift, and that I might not be half dead after all."

Her children had no idea how hard the chemo had been on her. She'd tried to shield them from it. There were enough things wrong in their lives, she didn't want to add a mother who complained about every ache and pain to their list of problems.

"You're not in bed?" Juliann asked, as that had become the normal.

"No. It's nine o'clock, and I've been up for an hour. Feeling good."

"Oh, Mom! I'm so happy to hear it."

"Thanks. It's been a long, dark winter, but I'm excited about spring, not just because I'm feeling better, but because it feels like a new chance."

"It *is* a new chance, mom." It wasn't hard to hear the happiness in Juliann's voice. Of course she was happy for her mom.

June smiled, watching the water drip from the faucet. She'd ask her husband to fix it at the end of last summer. He still hadn't gotten around to it. That and the light over the sink. She did know how to take the cover off, and it had been burned out for a year. All winter it had felt extra dark in the kitchen because that light wasn't working.

Juliann gave her an update on her classes, talking about some of the things she and her friends had been doing, and June listened, not looking at the dripping water, because she didn't want to be irritated.

"Then, Chad and Brandon helped me get that new couch I told you about into my apartment."

"I thought your dad was going to help you?" June said, her eyes going to the calendar that was held up by a magnet on the refrigerator.

"You know dad. He didn't show."

June pressed her lips together, keeping in the words of frustration. It was far from the first time her husband didn't show when he had promised.

At least he hadn't stolen anything from her.

When his mother had died, she had named their three children in her will, wanting them to get anything that was left after her estate was settled.

Her husband was the executor of the estate, and he had claimed that there was nothing left once everything was settled. That's what he had told the children. June had seen the bank account, and knew that there had been close to half a million dollars in it, once the sale of the house went through.

She had assumed he would send it to the kids, and she'd talked to them about it, but Wayne had never sent the money on.

There was probably a way to get it, going through the court system, but none of the kids had been interested in suing their dad, as much as they would have loved to have had a six-figure start in life.

June wasn't interested in suing her husband, either, as much as she wanted to have her children have the money.

She appreciated the fact that her kids would rather stay out of court, but it had destroyed their relationship with their father. What was left of it anyway. With Wayne's moods, his tendency to go on profane yelling rants, and accuse his kids of not helping him when he needed it.

He did the same thing to June, and she'd been tempted over the years to walk out.

She just couldn't reconcile that with the fact that she made vows and said for better or for worse. She wasn't sure what she had thought the "for worse" was going to be, but that sure seemed like it qualified.

"So...is dad helping you at all around the house?" Juliann said after she had finished talking about the last test she'd had in psychology and how she'd gotten the best grade in the class.

"He's your dad. Still the same." June didn't want to complain. She tried hard not to talk to the kids about how terrible their dad was. They knew it, first of all, and secondly, he was their dad. She didn't want to malign him to the people who were supposed to love him anyway.

"Mom, you know no one would blame you if you left him." Juliann's words were soft, and there was caring underlining each one.

"I know," she said, her words soft as well. Her two older children had said the same thing to her multiple times. No one who had been on the receiving end of one of Wayne's tirades, knowing that he was usually absent and didn't seem to care much about her except when he needed her, would blame June if she walked.

There were very few people who would blame her after seeing how he had neglected her through her cancer, or who knew how he treated her for most of their marriage.

"You're probably standing in the kitchen watching the sink drip," Juliann said with a bit of a smile in her voice. Her words wrapped around her like a warm hug, knowing someone cared to know her enough to know what she'd be doing.

"I am deliberately not looking at the sink dripping," June said, allowing her voice to sound like she was smiling as well. After all, she would far rather laugh at life's problems, than get down by them.

The Lord allowed her to go through the trials. Nothing came to her life without going through Him first, so if she was dealing with them, it was with His permission, and with His expectation that she would do her very best to go through it in such a way that He would be glorified.

She knew she didn't always do it as well as she could, but she kinda thought that God would far rather her be laughing than complaining.

"Maybe that sink is God's way of telling you that He wants you to be a little more independent. There's no reason why you can't call a plumber."

Juliann's words hit June's ear hard. She'd always allowed her husband to do the home repairs. But...why couldn't she call a plumber?

She had told Wayne about it, and he said he would fix it. He hadn't. How long did she have to wait before she made a phone call?

She straightened, then deflated.

What did she know about calling a plumber? Wayne had always handled the repairs in the home. True, usually things were broken for a really long time before he got around to fixing them, if he ever did, but...why not? She didn't have to sit around waiting.

"Didn't you say your new business was taking off? You have a little bit of money of your own now, right? You could call and handle it yourself."

"You're right Juliann. I never thought about that it like that. Maybe God really does want me to step out a little and be more independent."

By nature she was independent. She had never had to go in the same direction as everybody else. After all, if she had needed to do that, she would have been divorced long ago.

She really didn't know anyone who would have stayed in a marriage like hers. But, she'd stayed because she'd said she would. When she gave her word, she meant it and would keep it.

Keeping her word was a part of her identity, and the idea that she might break it made her feel like her word couldn't be trusted anymore. It wasn't so much what other people would think of her, as much as it was what she would think of herself. She didn't want to be someone who made vows, then broke them.

But, she kind of liked the idea of being someone who depended on God; someone who could call the plumber herself instead of waiting for her husband.

"While you're calling a plumber, why don't you look up a handyman, and see if you can get someone to fix that light. You used to use it all the time when I was growing up. I'd come down stairs in the morning, and you'd be sitting at the bar right beside the sink, using that light to read your Bible."

"That's true. I loved that light. It's just perfect in the morning, not too bright, but enough for me to be able to read by."

"So call someone and get it fixed, Mom. You can do it. You don't have to leave Dad, but you don't have to be more miserable than necessary."

Her daughter's words seemed wise, although June really liked the idea that maybe it was the Lord nudging her to be a little more independent. Maybe He wanted her to learn how to do things on her own.

After all, it hadn't seemed to be in His plan for her to have a fun and loving relationship like she'd always dreamed about. A relationship built on mutual respect and caring for her partner. Having someone she could depend on, not just someone who expected her to be available when he wanted her, but someone who wanted to spend time with her. Who wanted to be with her and to do things together.

That was never going to happen, and she could sit around regretting that, being sad, missing her kids who had filled that void in her life for so long, or, she could move forward with her life, fixing the things that irritated her, like a leaky faucet and a lightbulb that needed to be changed, or, she could continue to be miserable.

It seemed obvious which one God would want her to do.

"Juliann, I appreciate your wisdom. I've never even considered that the leaky faucet might be God's way of telling me something. Thank you for being willing to say something to me."

"I know you've always told me that I have to choose happiness, and I know you know that, too. I know too, going through cancer makes it hard to choose to be happy. But, God has something beautiful for you, Mom. I know he does. Maybe there are just a few lessons you have to learn yet."

Juliann's voice was quiet, but hopeful. There was a little bit of suppressed excitement in it, too, like she really believed June's life could be beautiful.

Maybe there really was an amazing relationship waiting for her. Maybe God was going to change Wayne's heart. Maybe he would see the light, and as he got right with God, he would want to be right with his wife, too. After all, he could hardly love God and serve Him, without being more loving and considerate to the people around him. It would be a natural byproduct of a life used to serve the Lord.

She hadn't felt this encouraged in a long time. As she hung up, after a few more words with Juliann, she looked around the kitchen, narrowing her eyes and nodding her head.

God had provided her with a little bit of extra money. She'd had to set up her own account online, one where her funds from her online business were deposited into, and Wayne didn't have access to them until she moved them to one of their accounts.

It was there for her use. And, with Juliann's words, a peace had settled down on her.

She smiled, then swiped her phone again, pulled up a search engine and typed in "plumbers."

Chapter 11

Darby hurried to the church, eager to see what had happened between Jonah and Amber.

Did they like each other? Were they getting along?

She wasn't sure whether it was a good sign that they were going to the church.

They had spent more than an hour and a half at the auction barn, so she thought that was good, but sometimes Amber liked to play the piano when she was upset, or scared, or nervous.

It calmed and soothed her. It was like a security blanket was to other kids. Or she didn't know what to compare it to for other eight-year-olds. Just...playing the piano did something for Amber that nothing else could, and she did it when she was feeling emotional.

Going up the front steps of the church, Darby could hardly believe that they left it open, but the doorknob turned easily in her hand, and she stepped into the vestibule. Going through the double doors and into the sanctuary, she could hear the piano's strains as soon as she walked in, and smiled.

Amber was playing her favorite. Bach.

Jonah stood against the wall, watching her, his face tilted toward Amber, but Darby could still see it.

He was entranced.

That wasn't hard to see.

Amber's playing had that effect on people.

Nerves swirled in her stomach.

Would he hear her and decide she needed to be out in the world? Would he tell her she shouldn't be hiding a talent like that? That she had been wrong in trying to let her daughter have a childhood?

If Jonah was going to push for Amber to play the piano professionally, Darby wasn't sure she would be able to fight him.

She could fight Nora, because Nora had wanted to give her up. But Jonah hadn't had a choice. She wasn't sure that it would be right for her to fight him.

She tried to remind herself that she had every right to love Amber and to try to do what was right for her. She had adopted her, and Amber was hers.

She just didn't think it was right that Jonah hadn't had any say in it.

Still, she didn't know whether that would influence her to allow him to push her into doing something that she didn't think was right for Amber.

You're asking for trouble. Just breathe, pray, go over, and talk to him.

She was breathing and praying, when he saw her and stepped away from the wall, walking toward her.

That made her smile.

So much had happened that day, so much that revolved around Jonah. And she found herself admiring him more and more.

Just one day wasn't enough to show a person's true character or even their personality completely.

A person could live with someone for years and never see all the aspects of their personality.

"How'd it go?" he asked when he was close to her.

It made her feel good that he was concerned. That he wanted to know, that he asked.

"They said you were basically a paragon of virtue. That I was safe as a baby with you."

She was paraphrasing, of course, but it made him smile.

"Your daughter... My daughter... *Our* daughter," he emphasized the word "our." "She's...amazing. I can't even think of words. She's beyond words. And I'm not just talking about her piano-playing abilities. Those are blowing me away. I've never really been into this kind of music, but maybe it's just because I've never heard it played correctly. This is amazing. It just makes me feel things I didn't even know I could feel." He kept his voice low, pitching it under the happy and bright tune that Amber played.

She'd heard that Jonah wasn't much of a talker, but he didn't seem to have any trouble rambling on with her. He might be searching for the right words, but he wanted to talk to her. She liked that.

"I'm so glad you enjoyed it," she said, smiling at his excitement. "Sometimes you can tell her mood by what she chooses to play. She's not practicing a piece for herself or her teacher, and it sounds to me like she's in a good mood."

"I hope so. I think she had a good time. She didn't really seem like she wanted to go, but Elias was heading out, and I didn't want to abandon you to the ladies of the community center." He looked at her like that would be a fate worse than death.

"They actually were telling me how to raise chicks. I didn't know how much you knew, so I got Miss Helen's phone number, and she's going to help me if we need it."

"That's great. I talked to some guys about it some, but I've never done it. They have chicks at the hardware store right now. So, we could go get some, unless you want to wait until after we come back from The Cities with the piano?"

"The ladies said that getting the piano might be a two-day thing."

"We can make it that if you want to."

"It wasn't that I wanted to, they just said it was a long drive, and they seemed to assume that it would take two days."

"We could drive down Friday night after school, and if we started early Saturday morning, surely we'd be able to make it home by evening."

"I would think so." She liked that he was willing to throw some ideas out and talk about them and didn't just tell her how it was going to be done. "Did Amber enjoy the auction barn?"

"I think so. The girls disappeared, and I didn't see them again until I had to text her to bring her back. They were laughing and giggling with their arms around each other when I saw them again, so I'm guessing that she might have made some new friends."

"That's great. I'm glad that she'll know some people at school tomorrow."

"That's what she said."

That stopped her. So they'd talked. Not that she hadn't thought that they would, it was just she wasn't sure.

"Did you and she get along okay?" she asked, a little more hesitantly, because even though she was Amber's mom, she didn't want to be nosy. After all, he was her dad, and there was no reason for him to have to answer to her other than she had custody.

"I think so. We were able to talk, and she smiled at me and held my hand, and I feel like those are all good signs."

"I agree. Sounds good to me."

"But..." He looked back at Amber who had moved into a more complicated piece, playing with precision and emotion.

"Yes?" she prompted when he paused. Maybe he was worried that Amber would stop playing and overhear them. Her stomach clenched. Maybe something happened, and he needed to talk to her about it. "Typically, when she starts to play, she doesn't stop for a really long time. She gets lost in the music and just goes from piece to piece."

"Good to hear. I wanted to talk you about something important." He took a breath. "Do you think we have time to sit down and have a short conversation?"

For the first time since she'd met him, Jonah looked nervous.

She wasn't sure entirely what that meant, but she figured it didn't bode well.

Her own stomach clenched.

"Sure. I have all the time you want." She tried to keep her voice light and not show his words had affected her and scared her a little.

He nodded at a pew a few rows back, which gave them a little more privacy, as Amber began to play a softer, slower piece.

"That's really pretty," he murmured as she sat down, sliding over to give him plenty of room.

"It's one of my favorites," she said softly.

"I can see why. It's kind of romantic, too."

"Yeah. It's a good one to play at night. It doesn't exactly make you sleepy, but it does relax you."

"I agree. She does it very well."

Darby nodded, used to people being impressed with her ability. Even Jonah, who probably didn't listen to classical music much, if ever, seemed impressed.

Still, that didn't take her mind off the fact that he had something that must be pretty important to talk to her about.

Then a light bulb went off in her head. He probably wanted to tell Amber right away that he was her father. That would be fine. She thought Amber would be able to adjust to it. It was a lot for a little girl... Or maybe he wanted to share custody.

That concerned her a little more, but after the recommendation of the ladies at the community center, she felt like that might even be a good thing.

She wouldn't be alone anymore, and he would offer her a little protection from Nora if Nora decided to come after her. Surely it gave them a little more credence if the two of them were together against Nora.

Surely a judge would consider that if Nora didn't tell her husband she was pregnant and was going to abort the baby, which was a matter of record, he would take into serious consideration the fact that the adoptive mom and the biological dad were together sharing custody...

She was borrowing trouble, and she had to stop it. She tried to fix her thoughts on positive things, that everything was going to work out, that God would work everything for good, that she just needed to trust the Lord had a plan, that even if there were hard things to do, she would be able to get through them, because God would help her.

She ran those positive thoughts through her head as Jonah seemed to search for words.

She wished he would just say whatever it was and not keep her in suspense.

But she appreciated the fact that he didn't want to spit out words that weren't accurate, or well thought out, and was waiting to try to make sure he got the right ones. She tried to be patient while he did that.

"With you having custody and me being the father, and with Nora kind of lingering around the edges of the picture, I thought it might be a good idea if we think about the pros and cons of entering into a marriage of convenience."

Well.

Wow. She hadn't expected that. Where had she heard that ninety-five percent of the things that people worry about never actually happened?

This was certainly the case here, because she hadn't been on that trail at all.

"A marriage of convenience?" She shook her head. "What is that?"

Amber had gotten to a dark and stormy part of the piece, and the music seemed to suit her mood. She almost laughed at how appropriate it was.

This was no laughing matter.

The man in front of her had just said "marriage." But he hadn't said anything about love, and she'd just met him today. How could she marry someone she didn't even know?

"Well, a couple people in town have actually done this, where they decide that a marriage makes sense for both of them. My friend Smith and his wife, both had a half share of a ranch. In order to keep it, they either needed to get married, or they would lose it all. They had two weeks to decide. They'd never met each other before, and they decided that a marriage of convenience made sense. Of course, they ended up falling in love with each other, and it turned into a real marriage."

He didn't go so far as to say that was what he was expecting, and Darby had the feeling she needed to prompt him.

"Is that what you're thinking for us?" she asked, and she hoped that there wasn't any hope in her voice. Because she didn't want to consider such a preposterous idea. She really didn't.

She hadn't ever considered getting married at all, mostly because she needed for the man that she was married to to love her child as much as she did. There was no way she was going to marry someone who didn't think that Amber was the best thing that ever happened to him.

She didn't have to worry about that with Jonah. Jonah was Amber's father. And he would love her because of that. He was unique out of all the men in the world just because of that.

But did she really want to enter into a marriage with a man who wanted her because she was the mother of his biological child and that made things easier for him?

"To be honest, I'm not entirely sure. I guess I hadn't really thought about it too much other than to say that I thought it would solve some of our problems. Make things easier for us. Make things better for Amber. Give her more of a solid foundation. I hate the thought that my daughter has grown up without a dad." He put out a hand. "Not saying anything about you. I know you've done the very best that you can. But I'm here. And I want to do everything good for her. Anything that makes her childhood better."

"Me too. And not to argue with you about that, because I'm aware of the studies that say that a child who grows up in a two-parent home has a much better chance of success in life, not to mention they have greater feelings of being loved and supported by their parents, if they have two parents, who are their biological parents."

"Exactly. And I get that you're not her biological mom, but she doesn't know that."

"No. But if Nora were to show up, she might find it out. I've been twisting over in my mind the pros and cons of telling her. I should have done it when she was a baby, just raised her to say that she was chosen by me. And that I didn't give birth to her, but I wanted her so much that I chose her." She shook her head. Then let out a breath. "I don't know. Just something to let her know, to make sure that she knew and understood how much I wanted her. I don't ever want her to feel like she's not wanted."

The look on his face was thoughtful, sincere. "And, I guess... I don't really want you to feel like you're not wanted. I don't want you to regret going into a marriage with me, thinking that I'm just doing it for her. I... That's my thought. I'm not going to sit here and try to tell you that I'm in love with you or that I have any of those feelings, but I find you appealing and interesting, and I think what you've done with Amber is pretty amazing. I highly admire and respect you, and I know those feelings are real. So yeah, I guess what happened with Smith and Abrielle is what I'd like to see for us. Although, I can't guarantee it."

"Of course not. But I guess if we're thinking that we're trying to develop a relationship, I think maybe the foundation could be there."

"I know. I agree. I know you're not desperate, and I'm not either, but I do think it would be a good idea all around. I can't really think of any drawbacks, other than if you fall in love with someone else and want to leave."

"No. If I commit to a marriage, I'm not going to be looking around for someone else to fall in love with."

"Sometimes it doesn't matter if we're not looking around. Sometimes it happens when we're not thinking about it."

"If you make a commitment to a marriage, you can't allow those thoughts in your head."

She felt very firm about that. It wasn't a matter of being unable to control herself and her desires. It was a matter of determining what she was going to do before she entered into a situation where she was tempted to do something wrong.

"I think as adults sometimes we feel an attraction to someone that we're not married to. Whether you're married or not, those are times where you tell yourself, that's off limits for me. You turn your back and walk away. I do not buy into the idea of falling in and out of love. At least, not where it happens that someone in marriage says 'I don't love you anymore.' Because love is a choice."

"I hadn't thought about it quite like that, but I agree with you. You don't fall out of love. Because you don't fall in love to begin with. You feel an attraction for someone, and then you work on building a relationship with them, although in our day and age, a lot of times it's a physical relationship, which is the weakest possible kind of relationship."

"I agree with that, although I think the physical relationship is an important part of marriage. And...I wouldn't want to have a marriage without one." She couldn't believe she said that. She could feel her cheeks heating, but she meant it and wouldn't take it back.

Marriage wasn't just two friends who lived together. Marriage was friendship that was also intimacy, physical and emotional.

She kind of thought men were better at physical intimacy, and women were better at emotional intimacy, but both of them needed the other.

"I think maybe sometimes in unhappy marriages, couples don't give the other one what they need." She spoke softly, not meeting his eyes.

Chapter 12

Amber began playing "Sheep May Safely Graze" by Bach, and Darby said, "This is one of my favorites. It's by Bach."

"I've heard of him. I...don't know much about composers or this kind of music. I hope you and Amber are going to teach me."

"I didn't mean to change the subject. But she's playing my favorite music. I don't take that as a sign or anything—"

"Maybe it is a sign. Maybe it's a little push in the right direction," he said, smiling.

"Yes. Maybe. It's just such a huge decision. I guess I can feel how you felt when I dropped the whole 'you have a daughter' thing on you. Except this is a choice I have to make that's going to affect the rest of my life, my daughter's life...your life."

"Accepting the idea that I had a daughter, or rejecting it, was my choice."

"That's true. You didn't have to believe me. And I might have been lying. Except for your eyes."

She smiled. Sitting in the church, with his hat off, she could see his eyes clearly. They were the exact same color as Amber's, and the same play of emotions went over them.

"Nora might have been lying, but I knew you weren't. And you're right, I could see my eyes. Still, it was a choice. I can't say I was tempted to ever deny my daughter, but I knew it was going to change my life. There was that thought and the decisions about how I was going to handle it."

"You reacted to it beautifully. That's part of the reason I'm even considering this marriage of convenience idea. Because I felt like I figured out what kind of man you are right there. Where you didn't just want your daughter, but you really wanted her. Wanted to know her, wanted to be with her. And was aghast at what Nora had done."

"Yeah. I probably didn't even react quite as strongly as I wanted to. I was, and still am, angry. Angry over what she did. It was so wrong." He took a breath and breathed out slowly, like it was coming from his very soul. Then he said, "I found, though, that anger just punishes me. Nora isn't going to care that I'm upset with her, and it's not going to affect her behavior in the future. So I'm just wasting my time being angry. Therefore, I'm going to try to let it go. It's not like me getting upset with her is going to help anything."

"Such a great attitude. And it's so correct. I need to try to do that more. Because you're right. Anger just punishes me."

"That's probably why the Bible tells us to be angry and sin not. You can get angry. I don't think God expects us to have emotions and not feel them as humans, but He doesn't want us to stay angry. He wants us to realize that He is in control, and He will be the one to hand out the judgment on people. It's up to us to do right, for ourselves, and not worry about what other people are doing. Because we're not getting their reward or punishment, we're getting our own."

"That's exactly what I think. That to the best of my ability, I need to forgive and love. Without regard to what other people do. The problem is, sometimes forgiving feels like accepting and saying that it's okay. Like, what she did was perfectly fine, and I'm not upset about it at all. But me being upset doesn't show her that it wasn't okay. Does that make sense?"

"Yeah. And I think probably you touched on one of the hardest things to do as a Christian. One of the things I've been struggling with, although there's been so much happening today I haven't thought about it much. But I'm angry at what she did. It was wrong. I should have known. But I have to forgive. I have to let go, because for me to hold that in, and continue to hold it against her, just hurts me. It's like poison in my body."

"Exactly right. You have to let it go,"

"And God handles it."

"I actually think that letting it go frees God up to step out and handle things. But He requires us to forgive first. Once that happens, then His plan can truly be free to be set in motion."

They sat for a while, listening to the strains of "Sheep May Safely Graze" surge into "Jesu, Joy of Man's Desiring."

"I wonder if Amber is playing my favorites on purpose. This is another one I love. It's not a hard one, but it's just so lilting and really beautiful."

His eyes crinkled when he smiled as he looked down at her sitting in the pew. "She knows your favorites?"

"Yeah. Sometimes when she wants to butter me up so she can get something she wants, she'll go in and play all of my favorites, and I mean she plays *all* of them. Then she'll come back out and ask me. I'm such a pushover."

"The music moves you?"

"Amber playing moves me. That's for sure. I do like music too. But just hearing my daughter play does something to my heart."

"This isn't the kind of music I typically listen to, but if my daughter and my wife love it, I think I will become a lover as well."

"You're not gonna try to talk us into liking your kind of music?"

"Liking music is a personal preference. I also feel that maybe a lot of times we listen to music for our own pleasure, and we forget it's another way we glorify God. We forget, and use music to make ourselves happy, rather than playing music that glorifies the Lord."

"I agree with that. A lot of the music that is popular today is popular because it makes us feel good. Not that this music doesn't make you feel good, but it's not sensual, it's a... I'm not even sure how to explain it."

"More of a spiritual goodness. You can feel your soul being ministered to versus your flesh being ministered to by popular music."

"That's a good explanation."

They listened to the strains wrap around them, Darby closing her eyes and leaning her head back, thinking that the church was the perfect place, with the amazing acoustics, and the way it felt was spiritual and deep and pure.

"It's been about an hour. It might be a good idea for us to make her stop. She'll play all day if we allow her to."

"If I could play like that, I'd want to play all day too."

Darby opened her eyes and straightened. "Would you mind taking her down, maybe getting some ice cream, if you don't mind. I'd like to sit here and pray about this for a bit."

She was kind of surprised she asked that. She knew he wasn't suggesting that they wait and think about it but wanted to tell Amber today he was her father and then Darby and he would get married.

"I don't want to push you."

"You're not. Surely God has an answer. And if He says no, or if He says wait, I'll tell you. But I kind of feel like He's not going to, and it's me that needs to get on board with Him. Sometimes I can be a little slow."

"All right. We'll do that. I'll take Amber, we'll get some ice cream, and we'll hang out at the little park down the street a ways."

"I saw it. I'll spend a little bit of time here and then come down."

"All right." He took a breath and put his arms out on the back of the pew in front of him. "I'm serious. It's okay if you say no."

"All right. I don't think I would say yes if I felt like no was the correct answer."

"I appreciate hearing that. I wouldn't want you to."

He stood and slid out of the pew, walking up to the piano and waiting until the last strains of music faded away before he touched Amber's shoulder, bending down to talk to her.

Darby watched as he spoke with his daughter, and she loved the way his body language said he cared. The gentle touch, the bending in, the whisper in her ear. The little smile on his face, and the way she looked up at him, grinning and nodding.

Sometimes she didn't leave the piano willingly, but she slid out right away, grasping his hand and then coming back down the aisle.

"Mr. Jonah said it was okay for me to go get ice cream with him. He said you would come in a little bit."

"I will. You'll have to let me know if they have any good flavors."

"They have a ton of flavors, and I'm sure she'll find something she loves," Jonah reassured her.

Amber smiled again and practically skipped down the aisle with her hand in Jonah's.

The door closed behind them, and it was quiet and still in the church.

Memories of music still swirled around her, and the spirits of worshipers through the years seemed to echo in the walls.

She felt like she could feel the spirit of the Lord. Feel His presence.

She knew, when she was outside, in her car, or at her house, God was always beside her. He was omnipresent, everywhere at the same time. She didn't understand how that could be, but she also didn't understand how stars could be millions of light-years away. So, just as she didn't question the idea of the stars being that far, she didn't question the idea of God being omnipresent. She didn't understand either one, but both were facts.

Still, in the church, and maybe in this church in particular, she could feel more. He was always there, no doubt, but sometimes with everything else that was going on, with people around, their problems, and that hustle and busyness of the day, the presence of the Lord and her feeling of it got pushed away.

She sat, quiet, just in silent worship, because she couldn't feel the presence of the Lord and not want to worship Him.

After a while, she just said simply and softly, "Lord, what should I do?"

His presence was still there, but she didn't detect any answers.

She knew sometimes God didn't answer right away. Sometimes He made her wait on His answer. To develop her patience, to develop her faith. To see if she was really going to trust Him or just move ahead and do the wrong thing.

Sometimes she'd done that. Moved ahead with her own thing.

But she didn't want to. Anytime she had, she'd regretted it, and even when she'd done something she knew she shouldn't, she'd always, deep in her heart, really wanted to do God's will. Often it was like truly wanting to eat vegetables but eating ice cream instead.

"Lord?"

Still nothing.

Please, Lord. I want to do the right thing. I want to do what You want me to do, I don't want to make a huge mistake. Please show me. Give me a sign or just let me know for sure that this is something that I need to go through.

She lingered in the silence a little more, waiting.

Amber was her main concern. After doing the Lord's will. Would having a marriage of convenience be best for her?

If things worked out between Jonah and Darby, it certainly would be. And Jonah seemed like the kind of man who would make sure that things worked out. He might never love her, but wasn't that her maybe hoping for more than what she needed? She just needed a stable, dependable man beside her. One who was willing to be a father to Amber.

And she had that in Jonah. Would she hold out, hoping that she would get more? And would she want to marry a man who wasn't Amber's father while Jonah was trying to be in the picture with Amber?

That seemed like it would make for a convoluted family.

Maybe that's why she had been so at peace with the idea. It should have shocked her, revolted her, and horrified her, the idea of marrying a man she just met.

But it would definitely be the best thing for Amber.

And while Jonah had given her some kind compliments, his concern seemed to be for Amber as well. Would it be wise if both of them thought they were doing the best thing for their daughter?

With that thought, a peace filled her soul. Like the idea was the exact right one.

When she lived for other people, and made decisions based on their welfare, on the best thing for them, God often rewarded her with benefits for herself. She knew that, and the idea gave her assurance.

She would make the best decision for her daughter, and she would assume that God would handle the rest.

Chapter 13

"All right, Amber," Darby said. "Say good night to Mr. Jonah and Mr. Gideon. And you and I are going to head upstairs."

Jonah glanced at Darby. They'd finished supper a couple of hours ago, and they'd been sitting in the living room, just chatting, with Amber coloring and playing with puzzles that Darby had packed.

Darby had promised him after she got done at the church, they would talk after Amber went to bed.

She hadn't given any clue as to what conclusion she'd come to, and he found his hands sweating and his stomach twisting all day long

"I'll see you in a bit?" he said after Amber had bid them both good night and started prancing up the stairs.

Darby nodded.

He watched her go, her movements graceful and confident. She wasn't arrogant, and she wasn't indecisive either. Neither did she seem like she needed anyone.

He supposed she'd been on her own for so long that she probably didn't.

He admired that, while it intimidated him as well.

"What's going on between you two?" Gideon asked low, even though they could hear the water running upstairs and most likely neither one of the girls could hear. "Did you tell her what you said you were going to?"

Gideon was known as being a goof-off, but he could also be serious. There was no hint of humor on his face, and Jonah knew that he really only wanted the best for them.

He could ask Gideon to leave to give them some privacy when Darby came back down, but he didn't want to put his friend out.

If she came back down, they could go outside and walk. It was still spring and cool at night, but it was clear, and the moon was almost full, and it might be a good setting for a conversation about marriage. Even if she was going to let him down.

"I did."

"What did she say?"

"We're supposed to talk once Amber's in bed."

"I can head out? Give you guys some space?" Gideon said immediately, but Jonah put his hand up.

"Stay. I'll take her outside. We'll take a walk, and that way you won't get stuck outside if the conversation lasts longer than I think it's going to."

"You think she's gonna turn you down?"

"Your guess is as good as mine."

He didn't know what that meant exactly, other than Gideon could read her just as well as he could. It wasn't like either one of them had known her longer than one day.

"I don't know what I was thinking. You don't meet a woman in the morning and offer to marry her that afternoon. I'm possibly the dumbest man on the planet."

"Am I supposed to argue with that?" Gideon asked. "Because I really don't feel like I have anything to say."

"Thanks. That's really sweet of you."

"Sweet. That's just what I've always wanted my good friend to call me. Sweet. One day with her, and all of a sudden, you turn into some kind of weirdo I don't know. You know it. If you think sweet is a compliment, just don't say anything if you can't say something nice."

Gideon grinned and turned the page on his magazine.

"It was a stupid idea. We're not even going to be home this summer. What was I thinking?"

"Pretty sure we've already gone over this. I agree. You're stupid. I don't know what you're thinking. If you don't know what you're thinking, I definitely don't know, and I'm pretty sure that if Darby has any sense at all, her answer is going to be no, so you don't have to keep kicking yourself about it."

"All right. That's a good point."

It was a point he wanted to adhere to, and so he determined he'd stop thinking about it and just patiently wait until Darby came back downstairs.

Except, he couldn't patiently wait.

He got up, wanting to pace.

He'd already done the dishes, right after supper while everyone else was settling into the living room.

Walking out to the kitchen, he looked out the window, into the dark night, and saw exactly nothing, then walked back out through the living room to the front door.

He shoved his hands in his pockets, then retraced his steps.

He figured he was probably driving Gideon nuts, but he owed Gideon, since there had been plenty of times where Gideon's joking and teasing had driven him crazy.

He must have made the trip from the window to the front door and back one hundred times before Darby finally showed up at the top of the stairs, coming down slowly.

She waited until she was at the bottom of the steps before she spoke. "I don't think she's quite asleep, but if Gideon doesn't mind keeping an ear out for her and maybe yelling for us if he hears her, I can talk to you?"

He was on his way back through the living room and had stopped in his tracks when he saw her, watching her walk down.

He turned his head, looking at Gideon.

"I'll give a holler, if I hear her or if she comes down."

"I think she'll be fine. She's not usually scared at night, but this is her first night in a new place, and I don't want her to be frightened."

"Of course not. I'll let you know," he promised again.

Darby still didn't seem like she relaxed, but she nodded her head and then raised her brows at Jonah before she walked to the door where her coat hung on a peg.

"I assume I'm going to need this?" she said as she grabbed her coat. "And I guess I should ask if it's okay if we go out?"

"I've actually told Gideon that's what we'd do. He offered to go instead, but I thought it'd be better for us."

"Yeah. I don't want Amber to hear anything until we decide what we're going to tell her."

"Good thought."

They didn't say anything more, but she finished putting her jacket on and walked out.

He almost grabbed his, but he'd acclimated to the cool North Dakota air, and he figured it would probably feel good, so he walked out with just his flannel on.

She waited for him at the top of the porch steps. He closed the door and moved over beside her.

"Anyplace in particular you want to walk?"

"You're the one that knows the property."

"All right, let's go over behind the barn, there's a field road that goes back to our hayfield and beyond. With as bright as the moon is, we should be able to see things clearly, and that's a nice walk."

"All right. I'll take your word for it."

He almost took her hand. He wanted to. It would be nicer to walk in the moonlight if he had that connection with her, but he didn't want to overstep. And he hadn't heard what her decision was about their marriage. It might be presumptuous of him to do that, plus, it would be awkward if she was going to tell him no, and there he was holding her hand.

She seemed confident and hadn't seemed hesitant or afraid.

Whatever decision she'd made, he got the feeling that she was totally at peace with it.

"Thanks for giving me that time in the church this afternoon. I needed it."

"I don't think it's ever going to be a hardship for me to spend time with my daughter. I enjoyed eating ice cream with her. I found out her favorite flavor is chocolate peanut butter. I was a little aghast, but I think I can train that out of her."

She laughed, as he had intended for her to do. He didn't want this to be all serious; whether she said yes, whether she said no, he wanted them to be able to be friends.

Tell her.

"Before you say anything, I wanted to say something."

"All right." She didn't sound irritated, just curious.

"Whatever your decision is, I want you to know I want to be friends with you. I like you, and we have Amber in common. I think, regardless of how things play out, it's important for us to remember that."

"That actually played into my decision. Your desire to do the right thing for Amber. Me...as a woman." She smiled a little sheepishly, maybe a whimsical smile. He was grateful for the full moon that allowed him to see that on her face. "I'm sure I'm not alone in saying that I have hopes and dreams, little romantic things that I think would be really nice."

They took a few more steps, and he didn't say anything. Wasn't sure if she was waiting for him to or just gathering her thoughts.

"But when you're a mother, I think it's important that the first thing you think about is your child."

"I agree. Same thing for a father. Even if you're new."

She laughed again. And he loved that she laughed easily, that she wasn't a diva who was hard to please or needed to be coerced into a good mood. That even with the serious discussion they were having, she could have fun and be happy.

"So, it was a little bit...hard...for me when you said that you wanted to get married just for Amber."

"But—"

"Wait."

He closed his mouth.

"Because it wasn't romantic, and it didn't suit my narrative about the way I wanted my marriage, my romance, to be."

"Okay." He knew it. He knew he hadn't done a very good job of showing her that he cared. And how could he? He'd just met her.

"But as I thought about it, I thought that was a good thing. After all, you're putting your daughter first. And while I think that when two people are married, their relationship should come before anything else, after all, they pledged themselves to each other, and children will come, and then they leave, but your mate stays with you forever. For a lifetime. Until death."

"That's true."

"So, in a marriage, you should put each other first, and then your children."

"I agree with that," he said softly. He figured she was telling him that he had done it all wrong. And while he didn't exactly agree, since they weren't married yet, he understood what she was saying.

"After you left, and I was sitting in the church alone, just thinking, the thought that came to me as I was going over everything that had been happening was that I loved that you were more concerned about her than you were about yourself. That said a lot to me about your character and how you were going to parent."

He liked what she said. It made him feel good. Made him think that even though she was going to turn him down, she wanted to do it gently, letting him know that it wasn't because of anything he had done wrong.

It was good to know.

"And I realized that if you had put me first, and our relationship, and tried to convince me that you had somehow fallen in love with me in the space of six hours and wanted to marry me the same day you met me, it would have gone over really terribly. I wouldn't have believed a word. You would have sounded insincere, and even though there are words that I would like to hear, words of romance and compliments that a man tells the woman he loves, they were out of place today."

He waited. His breath shallow.

"Instead, naturally, without thinking about it, because you didn't have time, you said the exact thing that you should have said. That we needed to put the well-being of our daughter first. And that's why you wanted to have a marriage of convenience. I... I want more than just convenience, but I don't want that today. I want that...eventually."

"I should have waited."

"No. The very best thing for Amber is for her mother and her father to be married. I'm willing to do that. Tomorrow if you want. I...am a little scared, but I have a huge amount of peace about this decision. There aren't too many decisions I've made that I felt so sure about. But as I was sitting in the church, it just felt like the very right thing. And if you're willing, I am too."

He didn't know what to say. He hadn't been expecting it. He had talked himself into the idea that she would think he was crazy, because it was a crazy idea.

But what she said was right, and it was what he wanted too. They seemed to be at least compatible when it came to Amber. And, for now, she needed to be first.

"I'm ready to do it tomorrow if you want," he finally said, letting the words come out easily. She was scared? He was nervous too. To become a father today, a husband tomorrow... It totally changed everything he had been planning for his life.

He couldn't back out on Gideon now, not for this summer, but he wasn't going to be able to continue to travel for work. He couldn't do that and leave his family at home.

Maybe that was okay for some people, but not for him. To him, that was just a recipe to have the relationship grow cold, and to have someone be dissatisfied, and for him to lose the most important thing in the world to him, and that was his family.

The family that he didn't even know he had yesterday.

"I'm gonna need to make some changes in my life. I can't make them right away, but a married man can't run around and never be home. I... I already have plans for the summer, but we can talk about what we're going to do. I can't keep going away and leaving you home by yourself, alone with our daughter."

"I can't say that I'm excited about being alone in a strange place, in a strange state, where I knew no one, and where I'm completely isolated out here, but I have to say that being in Sweet Water today...it feels like it's not just a community, but it's an extended family. I know I'm going to be okay."

Her words were brave, but he knew she meant them.

"Sweet Water is a unique town. And I'm sure you will be just fine. There might even be someone who will come out and stay with you if you want that."

"No. I think I would like a dog, at least one, and one that barks a lot. But otherwise, I think I'm going to enjoy it here. It's peaceful and beautiful, and I just feel like I've come home. It's a hard thing to explain, but it's the truth. I just feel complete peace about the direction of my life right now, like God is guiding it, and I'm just following along with wherever He's leading, and I like it. I wish I had been this confident about God leading the rest of my life."

"Yeah. It's really nice when you can see God's hand all over things and just know you're doing the right thing."

"Yeah."

Chapter 14

D arby paused. Then she said, "Are you okay with all of that?"

"Yeah. I want to do some thinking, and I need to talk to Gideon and to Zeke and Baker and make sure that they're on board with everything. You're still going to be working in the business?"

"Yes. I was planning on doing the books as long as you want me."

"All right. Gideon said he would move out to the other house that we have. It's not as nice, and it needs some work, but that would give him something to do while he's back, and it would give you and me and Amber some privacy. Since we don't know each other very well, it might be nice to just have some time without other people popping in, where we can talk to each other and get to know each other."

"I appreciate that. I... I think it's going to be a hard summer. Because you're right, I don't want to get married to someone just to have them disappear. And it's kind of pointless to tell Amber she has a father and then have the father never be around. But I'm used to being a single mom. It's not like this is going to be something new for me."

"That's a good point. And what you said kind of brings me to my other thought, and that is...when are we going to tell Amber that I'm her dad?"

He held his breath while he waited for her answer. He didn't want to wait a long time. He wanted to step right into that role and make up for lost time. But it was also clear to him that Amber had been dealing with a lot of changes, and adding that to her life, along with a new state and a new school, a new house and new surroundings, probably wasn't the best thing for her.

Darby looked up at the stars, biting her lip. His eyes caught on that, and he almost forgot to listen as she started to speak.

"Let's let her get to school first, I'll take her in the morning and get her registered, and we'll see how the first day goes. If she comes home happy, with things going well, maybe we should tell her. Or we could wait till Friday, before we go to pick out a piano, so that if it upsets her, she'll at least have music with which to soothe herself. Although we'll have to wait for a while until the piano is actually delivered. The one I bought in Baltimore, I had to wait a week. But I'm guessing that Baltimore might be slightly different than North Dakota."

"Probably." He grunted. "Slightly, anyway. And this one will come from The Cities, so it's quite a drive. They'll probably have to put it on the schedule."

"But she'll be able to play while we're picking it out. That will be good for her."

"We can always take her to church if she needs to play before it comes." It was interesting that the piano was what she needed in order to soothe herself.

He supposed if he had a talent like hers, he would want to play as well.

"All right, I guess once you leave in the morning, I'll call the preacher and see if we can get something set up. He... He's probably used to this kind of thing, because this isn't the first marriage of convenience he's done this year. In fact, he's done several over the last few years."

"That's kind of crazy, that such a small town has so many marriages of convenience. And it's even more crazy because when I stopped in town today, I definitely did not expect to be talking about getting married tonight."

"When I saw you cowering behind the bench, scared to death of Billy, it wasn't my first thought, either."

"I was not cowering," she said, smiling at his description.

Their eyes met in the moonlight. He wanted to reach over and take her hand.

He teased her instead. "Of course not. You were just scrunching down behind there, because you were doing your deep knee bends for the day."

"Hey. You gotta get your exercise in whenever you can."

"Yes. Cows inspire me to exercise as well."

"Maybe we should get a whole herd of them, then, because we want you to stay healthy."

"I don't know, I've seen how one cow inspires you to exercise. I can't imagine what an entire herd would inspire you to do."

"All right. We've got to get something straight here."

"Yeah?" he asked, a smile still lifting his lips. If they could joke with each other, he thought they were going to be just fine.

"You are not allowed to make fun of me for being afraid of the cow. It was the first time in my life I ever came face-to-face with a real, live, not-fenced-in cow, and if that had been you, you would have been scared too."

"No. I don't think so. I didn't grow up around cows, exactly. But it was rural Indiana, so I did see cows, but Billy was my first experience as well, and I did not hide behind a bench when I first saw him."

"Probably because there were no benches to hide behind."

He laughed. "All right. That's probably true."

Her laughter joined his, and they continued to walk. He supposed he could have suggested that they turn around. They'd finished talking about everything that he wanted to. But he kind of wanted to get to know her.

"What did you make in your catering business? Did you have specialties?"

"I did. I actually still have the recipes. Everything is saved on my laptop. But I handed everything over to the person who bought it. They even took over my website. It was a hard decision, and I still miss it some."

"I was just about to ask that. We're kind of rural out here, and I don't know if a catering business would work, but—"

"I'll be happy as a bookkeeper. I'll love it. If not the work, I'll love the freedom, that I can choose my own hours, that I can take work or do it another day at my leisure, but being here, being able to work in the same house where Amber will be all summer, is perfect. It was hard sometimes to find a sitter when I had to cater a wedding or in the spring when I had a lot of bridal showers and baby showers and even some business dinners. Awards nights. Even some school functions. Although, my prices were a little out of their price range. I did a prom night once. That was pretty special."

"I can't even imagine. That would have been crazy. All those teenagers."

She smiled, a little dreamy, he thought. "They were all dressed up. They all had stars in their eyes, with their suits and ball gowns, or whatever they wear nowadays. It was just fun."

He could hear the smile in her voice as she described her happy memories.

It made him wish that he'd been there. But he liked the idea that she had made up her mind that whatever she was doing, she was going to enjoy it. That was a good decision.

"What about you? You were in the Air Force?"

"Yeah. That's how Gideon and I met. And Elias was our crew commander. We ended up in a hostage situation together, which really bonded us all. Smith was part of it too, although he's married and lives a few miles away, and then Baker and Zeke who are coming out sometime, maybe, if they ever get around to it. We were all on the same crew."

"What's holding the other two up?"

"I guess you know, since you sold everything and moved. It took you a year to get everything in line. I suppose that's what's going on with them."

"It's harder when you have kids."

"Yeah. But neither one of them are married, so it's not that, it's just getting things wrapped up so that they're free to go. North Dakota isn't exactly close to anything, so once you're here, it's a drive to get anywhere else."

"I see."

"But if they come out this summer, they can help us with the work. I might be able to be home a little bit more."

"I'm not worried about it. I don't like it, but I'm not worrying."

"I guess I just feel like I'm taking on a pretty big responsibility, and I'm not doing a very good job if I'm not even going to be there to take care of my family most of the time."

"But you will be there. And you're doing the right thing. And if you didn't marry me, I would be here by myself."

"I know. But when I'm your husband, it's a little bit different."

"All right. I agree with that. A husband should be different than just any Joe off the street."

"Thank you. That's what I thought."

They took a few steps in silence. He had a bunch of questions rolling around in his head. There wasn't enough time for them to really get to know each other, but he could ask a few.

"Is that what you went to college for? Restaurant management?"

"Yeah. It is. And I worked a little bit in a couple of high-end restaurants around Baltimore before I launched my own catering business. It was a bit of a risk, but I knew that I would have more time to spend with Amber, if I did. At least, I'd be able to pick and choose my hours a bit more."

"That was smart."

"I don't know. It was definitely a risk. It worked out, but I was scared it was going to fail. So many businesses do. Still, when I was launching that, I had the same calm assurance that I have right now."

"I like that. I guess maybe your calmness is rubbing off on me. I'm not worried about it either. Actually, I was more worried you were going to tell me no."

"Are you serious? I could have told you that I was going to tell you yes right away. I just... I wanted to explain things. I spent most of the day trying to think of exactly what I wanted to say. Because, once we take this step, it's not something I want to undo. Ever."

"I don't plan to undo it, either. I would still be married to Nora, even though I don't really care for her and realized I had made a mistake not long after we were married. But she left me."

"I believe that. You seem like the kind of guy who's pretty steady and would stick with things."

"I like to think I am anyway."

"I know where you met your buddies, but what made you join the Air Force? You like to fly?"

"I do. Maybe we can go for a flight together at some point."

"I think I'd really like that."

"Our plane is just a two-seater, so I wouldn't be able to take Amber when I take you. She has to have her own ride. We use the plane for work, so it's not something I'm going to be able to do a lot, but I know the guys wouldn't care at all. It's...addicting."

"That's what you always wanted to do?"

"Yep. I mean, when I was a kid, I wanted to fly commercial airlines. And as I grew older, I realized that you had to have so many hours before you do that and a progression of aircraft you're certified to handle, so the Air Force looked like the best thing for me. But once I got in there, I ended up working on planes rather than flying them. Which was a disappointment, but not a huge one.

I guess it's maybe like being able to work on your own car. When you love cars, it's fun to work on something you love."

"Did you eventually fly planes in the Air Force?" she asked, sounding a little unsure.

"That's not quite the way it works. But no. I eventually saved up enough money to pay for lessons and got my private license. I worked on getting hours on the side, during my free time. It was a labor of love. I got way more hours than I needed, and I aced my license exam. And my instrument exam as well. But sometimes your passion doesn't pay the bills, and I haven't flown nearly as much as I would like to."

"Then you should look for a job that requires flying?"

"Crop dusting does. That's kind of what we wanted to do. But there are other things to go along with that."

"But I meant, like someone hires you to fly. And that's all you do. Like a pilot."

"That's a possibility, I guess. There aren't very many airports close though, so we'd probably have to relocate. But I don't know, the idea of working with my buddies, and being out here, just trying to make it on our own, that appealed to the adventurer in me."

"That's funny. I don't think I have any adventurer in me. I want things to be safe and calm and never experience even a ripple."

"Maybe you'd better do something other than life, because I don't know anyone's life that is safe and calm and never has a ripple."

"I know, right? Heaven's going to be great. No drama for eternity. I am so down for that."

"But each issue, problem, adventure you face, each one you get through, makes you stronger. You learn how to handle things, learn your weaknesses, and can work on trying to shore them up with Bible verses, studying Scripture and taking it and applying it to the areas where you know you need work."

"That's a good way of looking at it. I guess my way of looking at it is I try to avoid it as much as possible, because I hate being scared and uncomfortable."

"I suppose that's one way." He laughed a little with her, since they both knew it wasn't a good way.

"But I know your way's the best. It's makes for a smarter life."

"It makes for a life with a lot of work anyway."

He figured it had probably been about an hour, and they ought to head back.

"Gideon hasn't texted me, but I think we probably ought to head back."

"I think that's a good idea. It's a little bit chilly, and you have to be cold."

"I think you kind of acclimate to the cold. And honestly, this doesn't feel that bad to me. Also, I was kind of nervous, and I knew those nerves would keep me warm. I wasn't too concerned about it." He paused and then continued. "In the winter, things can get dangerously cold. You definitely have to watch out for that here. That's probably the thing about North Dakota. If you can handle the winters, the darkness and the cold and the wind—the wind drives a lot of people crazy—then it's a good place to live."

"If I can't handle the winters, are we going to go somewhere else?"

"Yes." He didn't have to hesitate to say that. If she was his wife, and she couldn't live where he had chosen, for whatever reason, he would be moving. He wasn't going to make her stay someplace that she hated or that made her uncomfortable or made her life more difficult. "I'm not sure where we'll go, but we'll go somewhere, because I do not want you to be unhappy."

"I believe you can choose to be happy wherever you want to be."

"I agree with that, but we don't have to stay in a place where every day you wake up and pick up your cross and try to pretend to be happy, until you actually feel it. We can go somewhere else."

"That's a good thought. Thank you for that. I hope it's not necessary."

He grunted, thinking that if his impression of her was any indication, it probably wouldn't be. Because she would decide to be happy, and then she would do it.

Chapter 15

"**A**re you ready?" Amber asked, calling up the stairs to Darby who had made breakfast and now was trying to figure out what to wear.

Not that it mattered. She was just getting married. That was all.

But she hadn't been married before, and while she'd become a mom, she still had hopes and dreams about her wedding from when she was younger.

A pretty dress, flowers, being a princess for a day.

Those things seemed silly when she considered the importance of the occasion and realized that in her dreams, she'd never really thought about the lifetime vow she'd be making. The sacrifice required to get along with another human for the rest of her life, that living in close proximity with them was going to take.

Still, the occasion seemed to call for something nice, and she'd given away, put into storage, or sold almost everything she had in Baltimore.

She hadn't known where they were going to end up, and she hadn't wanted to haul a bunch of things around the country, if things with Amber's father hadn't worked out.

She certainly had never thought she'd be marrying Amber's father.

So, she was left with very few choices. Actually, not much choice. Maybe it was just nerves that were making her drag her feet.

"Mom?" Amber called up again.

"I know you don't want to be late, honey, but we have a few minutes yet." She had jeans, T-shirts, and one button-down shirt.

She had a jean skirt she'd brought to wear to church, and that was something she would pair with the button-down.

She had sneakers and a pair of cowgirl boots.

All of her winter clothing was still in storage as well.

There was plenty of money to pay for the storage...that was something else she needed to talk to Jonah about. The money.

He hadn't mentioned it, although she assumed he knew she had a good bit since she sold her business.

There weren't any stipulations on it, of course, but as a married woman, she would want to share the decisions for any finances with her husband. Not just hers, but she wanted him to share his decisions with her. That was normal, right?

So many things she needed to think about, and here she was dithering over her clothing.

A rap sounded on her door.

It didn't sound like Amber knocking.

"Come on in," she called, still standing beside her bed, looking down at her meager amount of clothing.

"I was thinking maybe you were thinking about changing your mind?" Jonah said before he was barely in, although he stepped further in then shut the door behind him.

"No. I haven't."

Not really. She was feeling cold feet, but she wasn't going to act on them. She'd made a decision, she had peace about it, she was going to move forward, no matter what the roadblocks were for her.

Jonah walked slowly around the bed toward her. He stopped when he was right beside her, and she thought maybe he would put a hand on her shoulder, touch her arm, but he didn't.

"You don't have to do this if you don't want to."

She took a deep breath, trying to steady her nerves, to make her voice sound confident, and to make her stomach stop clenching like she was checking into prison.

"I want to. I just...just had some things I was thinking about."

She hardly thought he'd be interested in the things she had been thinking, and she didn't want to bore him on their wedding day by talking about them.

"What are you thinking?" he asked.

She shook her head.

"You don't want to tell me? Or you can't?" he probed.

"Do you really want to know?"

"I'm not really in the habit of asking questions that I don't want to know the answers to. I know...I know a lot of times there are rhetorical questions, like how are you, what are you doing? But I never really understood what's the point of asking if you're not interested in hearing the answer. You know?"

"Oh. I'll keep that in mind."

"Do that. Because I'm serious. I want to know what you're thinking. Because I have no idea."

"What are *you* thinking?" she asked, still a little uncomfortable trying to share her entire heart, when she didn't know this man very well.

"I'm thinking I'm scared. Thinking this is a huge step. I'm thinking the pastor said he wants to do marriage counseling, and I'm hoping it doesn't talk you out of anything." He grinned a little, and she laughed.

"That's a funny thing to be scared about."

"A lot of times, our fears are irrational, aren't they?"

"That's a good point. I suppose you're right. I don't really have fears. I mean, I'm nervous."

"That's understandable."

"I guess... I guess I was just thinking about being a little girl, dreaming about my wedding."

"You want a wedding? We can plan something."

She loved that he asked that right away. He wasn't trying to talk her into it or tell her that she didn't really want what she actually wanted. But that he was willing to step aside from what he had thought was best and do what she didn't even think was best but was just what she wanted.

It's funny how that strengthened her resolve and her thoughts that she was doing the exact right thing by marrying him.

He wasn't going to just dismiss her. Act like her concerns were crazy. That she wasn't important, didn't matter. He was going to take her seriously.

Maybe it was that thought, along with the idea that she didn't have to wait for him to touch her.

She lifted her hand and put it on his forearm, which hung at his side. "Thank you for caring. That's what that feels like, anyway."

"Of course I care. If I'm going to marry you, it's my job to care about you."

"I don't need a big wedding. I guess I was just realizing the same thing you did, that it's a big step, and I was looking back before I took it, you know?"

"You used to want a big wedding?"

"I think every little girl dreams of being a princess. Of being admired and told she's beautiful, and to be a little spoiled, and that's what weddings turn into."

"You're saying that like you don't necessarily think it's a good thing," he said, and while she had been talking, his hand moved, making her hand slide down his forearm, and he had joined their hands together. Taking hers up in his and putting his other hand over top of it, like he was cradling it, protecting it.

It was perfect symbolism, because that's the way he had made her feel, protected and cherished.

"I guess when you're a little girl and you're looking at all the pretty things, that's where your eyes go, and they're just a distraction from what's really important. We... Maybe as a society, we have a tendency to place a big emphasis on the things that don't really matter and ignore or forget the things that do. I know, for me, when I was thinking about wanting to be a princess for a day, and that beautiful wedding gown that I would wear, and all the flowers in the church and all of those things, I never once thought about the commitment that was being made. The vows that would be spoken. The promises that I would have to keep. What a huge step in the life of someone that is. I guess I was all about the pomp and circumstance, and not about the substance underneath."

"It's okay to have pomp and circumstance. God went to great pains to describe how the temple was going to be built. He even went through great pains to talk about the tabernacle and how everything was set up as the Israelites were traveling through the desert. It was important to him that things were to be beautiful. He talks about the intricate carvings and the gold they used. Full chapters in the Bible are devoted to describing it. Surely that means that God cares about how things look, about making things beautiful?"

She tilted her head to the side, a little distracted by the way his fingers moved over her hand. She had to admit he had a point.

"Those are beautiful things to honor and glorify the Lord," she finally said.

"Don't you think a bride adorned for her wedding honors and glorifies the Lord? I think he refers to the church as a bride, looking beautiful for her groom."

"Okay. He does. That's a good point. So the idea of a bride looking beautiful on her wedding day is biblical. But we've taken all the Bible that we can out of it, taken the purity that day is supposed to represent and the joining of two lives, and just made it into something that's supposed to suit our fancy?"

"Well, maybe women have a tendency to go one way with it, to make it so big and beautiful and crazy that it's more like a fantasy than reality, and certainly no one's thinking about glorifying God. But I think men have a tendency to go the other way. Let's just show up in jeans and a T-shirt and get this thing done. And we don't think about glorifying God with beauty and grace and skill, either."

It was funny, the more she talked to him, the more she found things to admire. Because he wasn't just blaming women for leaving the Lord, he was allowing that his gender might have a problem with it as well.

"So I guess that's the whole point. The point of beauty and grace on her wedding day is about glorifying God, for the union that's supposed to take place. The vows which are going to be said, for the purity represented, and the couple that he joins from two people into one?"

"Now I think you have it." He grinned, looking abashed. "But it convinced me that maybe we should stop and do things a little differently."

"It's not a command, is it?"

"No. I think we do have a tendency to make it an idol when we overdo it. God doesn't say we have to do it."

"I think we should go ahead." She spoke with a decisive tone.

He grinned. "I like that. But I'm still not sure I understand what the holdup was? You were just thinking?"

"Yeah. I guess I was looking at my jeans and my jean skirt and thinking that I didn't have anything very nice to wear, and I guess I was thinking it was my wedding, and I wanted to look more like a bride and less like someone showing up for a rodeo."

"I will take you however you look. That's not an issue with me."

"I know. I wasn't really trying to impress you, although I guess every bride wants to feel beautiful."

Her words drifted off into the air, and he didn't say anything for a while. She wanted to laugh or do something to break the tension that seemed to have fallen, as he grew still, and then with the hand that wasn't holding hers, he reached out and touched her chin. Just a light touch, soft, gentle. He turned her head, until she was looking at him.

"You're beautiful."

That's all he said. He didn't try to explain anything, didn't try to talk her into it. He just spoke the words, two of them, like they were fact and not wishful thinking on her part.

She wanted to deny it. She knew no one else in the world would agree with him. She might pass as pretty once in a while, when she got herself all fixed up, but she was plain, ordinary, and trying to pretend otherwise was silly.

Except, when he looked at her like that, with the honesty and sincerity in his eyes, and something else, something a little darker, and the way he gazed steadily at her, the caring concern he had shown when he walked over and took her hand, the way he tilted her head to make sure she looked at him and saw him, and those two words, ones that warmed her heart and spread heat throughout her body—he made her feel beautiful.

She tried to smile, but her lips stumbled, because they couldn't quite stretch up.

And she didn't know what to say. She wanted to say something to shrug off the compliment; she didn't feel like she deserved it.

But she didn't want to make his words seem like they weren't important, or that she didn't care what he said.

Or that they didn't mean exactly what he wanted them to, to her. Not because his words changed her looks on the outside in any way, but they changed her on the inside.

How did she explain?

Finally, figuring she needed to say something, she murmured, "Thank you."

Her words made him smile, like he was concerned she was going to argue with him or that she didn't understand something.

Maybe she didn't, but she knew that whatever he did, he had her best interests at heart.

Funny that she had that confidence in him, when she hadn't known him that long.

"We can go somewhere to go shopping, if that's what you like?" he finally said, and the hand that had been on her chin dropped.

Maybe it was her imagination, but it felt like maybe he touched her skin for a second with a featherlight touch before his fingers moved away.

"No. I have tons of clothes in storage in Baltimore. I just hadn't anticipated the need to have anything fancy to wear. And I think fancy would be out of place anyway. I... I actually think jeans and a button-down shirt are exactly what I should wear."

"Are you sure?"

"Yes. If you give me two minutes, I'll get them on, and we'll be ready."

"All right. It's not a problem for me to go downstairs and hang out with Amber for a while, but I just wanted to make sure everything was okay up here."

"Thank you for thinking of me and for making sure everything was okay. And it is. It's perfectly okay."

That was true. It was. Talking to him, seeing his knowledge of the Bible, for one, which eased her mind more than she could say, and how he was willing to totally revamp their plans if she wasn't on board, had done more to eradicate any nerves that she had, and she found herself humming softly as she changed.

Her issue had been about what she wore, but he had come in and eased her mind about so many other things.

She couldn't help but think that that was just the Lord working through her future husband on her behalf on her wedding day. And she sent up a silent prayer of thanks.

Chapter 16

"Typically, when I do marriage counseling, I talk about the roles of the husband and wife in the marriage. But I think a lot of times, we forget that if we just apply Christian principles to our marriage, there will be no strife or discontentment there."

The pastor folded his hands together, his elbows on his desk, looking at Jonah and Darby over the rims of his glasses.

Jonah nodded. Out of his peripheral vision, he could see Darby nodding as well.

The man had a point.

Jonah hadn't been sure what to expect when the pastor had asked to do marriage counseling before he married them, and he had half expected him to tell them that they hadn't known each other long enough, and they were making a foolish decision.

But after making sure that they were both dedicated followers of Christ, he'd asked them to sit down and had opened his counseling with that statement.

Jonah felt himself relax a little.

"The Bible says 'Let no corrupt communication proceed out of your mouth,'" he lifted his brows, looking at both of them, and then he said, "'but that which is good to the use of edifying, that it may minister grace unto the hearers.'" He gave that a moment to sink in before he said, "The Bible also says in that same passage in Ephesians that we are to 'Let all bitterness—'" He paused after that word, and he seemed to be looking at Darby.

Jonah didn't think Darby held any bitterness, but maybe the pastor was thinking it was typically women who got bitter. He wasn't sure.

The pastor continued, "'—and wrath, and anger—'" He paused again and looked at Jonah this time.

Jonah was sure that was something that men had more of an issue with than women, but he also knew people of both genders struggled with anger issues.

"'—and clamor, and evil speaking, be put away from you, with all malice: and be ye kind one to another, tenderhearted, forgiving one another, even as God for Christ's sake hath forgiven you.'"

Again, the pastor paused, and Jonah thought about what a great speaker he was. He had been talking slowly, making eye contact, making sure both of them were listening.

"Right there is a passage, that if you both adhere to it, you are almost certain to be guaranteed to have a marriage that lasts for a lifetime."

He looked between them. "It takes both of you. But isn't that what husbands and wives should do for each other? Edifying, or lifting up, building up, encouraging, your spouse. The Bible commands you to edify other Christians, why wouldn't you do that for your spouse first? Use your words. Compliment them. Don't let a day, week, month go by where you haven't told them how wonderful they are, and don't just say general things. Tell them the specific things that they're wonderful at. Tell them the specific things you're thankful for. Tell them the specific things you think they do well. Tell them the specific things you appreciate about them." The man paused. "Don't do it so often that it becomes rote. That doesn't mean anything. That you're just flipping off words, and your spouse isn't feeling like you mean them. But then, something maybe we all have a little bit of trouble with, make sure your actions don't make your words into a lie."

He smiled a little. "If you tell her she's a wonderful cook, but you complain about supper, or you don't eat it, or you prefer to eat somewhere else, she's not going to believe that you love her cooking. I'm not going to believe that you love her cooking, no one is. You can't expect her to believe your lies."

Jonah lifted his head. Actions had to follow and back up words. In everything.

"If you compliment him on being a great provider, and then you worry about your finances, he's not going to believe that you think he's a great provider."

Darby nodded.

"But what if he isn't a great provider?" The pastor asked a rhetorical question, giving Darby a little smile. "Don't compliment him on that area, but don't complain about it, either. That passage says to build people up. Complaining about what they don't do right doesn't build them, it tears them down. Not to say that you can't have a productive conversation about your finances and what you're going to do to pay the bills, but complaining isn't something that should be involved in that conversation. Insults, belittling, saying you 'always,' or you 'never,' in a negative way. Those tear your marriage down. The Bible says a wise woman builds her house, and I often think that a wise woman knows that she probably builds it with her words, her actions, the way she supports her husband."

He lifted a brow at Jonah. "Same goes for you. If you want a happy wife, you can't complain about everything that she does. You can't even complain about a few things. Make it your mission, from this day out, to never say anything unkind, mean, belittling, or wrong about that woman beside you."

His eyes shifted back over to Darby. "You make the same determination about that man you have. He's a good man, but I guarantee you, he's got faults. He snores, he tells stupid jokes, he's immature sometimes, and he's going to mess up, or whatever his problems are. Whatever they are, even if they're character driven, go to the Lord about them. And make sure that you focus on his good parts."

"I often feel like the Lord had us focusing on these things, because He knows that whatever we think about, what we focus on, whatever we do, grows and gets bigger in our mind. If we look at other people, and we see their good parts, if we refuse to dwell on their flaws, we're going to see a really wonderful person. But if we look at them and think about all the things they do that annoy us, guess what's going to be really big in our minds?"

The pastor nodded along with Jonah and Darby.

"That's right. We're going to be irritated and upset with our spouses. We'll feel like we've been given the short stick, feel like there might be somebody else better out there who can do a better job, someone who would love us better, who would take care of us better, who would cook better or clean better or pay attention to us better. If you have issues, you can talk about them, but focus on the good. And do not allow yourself to think that there might be someone else anywhere who would be better. This is your choice. And like that game show said at one time, this is your final answer. The person beside you is your choice, your only choice, for the rest of your life."

He paused, as though waiting to see if they had any questions, or if one of them was going to get up and run screaming.

Jonah almost laughed at the thought, although he wouldn't be laughing if Darby would have done it.

He thought she was solid. He knew he was. She'd been different since the moment he'd seen her, and there hadn't been a single thing that she had done that had made him think that he was making a wrong decision here.

"The end of the last verse that I read to you—'be ye kind to one another, tenderhearted, forgiving one another, even as God for Christ's sake hath forgiven you,'" the pastor said, "is one other area

I want to touch on. This says be kind. It's a command. You are to be kind. And why would you not make your spouse the first person in your life that you're kind to? Of course we are supposed to be kind to all people, but your spouse comes first. Always. In everything. Be kind to them. Sometimes I feel like, for men especially, sorry, Jonah, that I need to spell out kindness."

He let out a long breath, as though he were thinking.

"Maybe we just want to pretend we don't know, I'm not sure. But if you can do something to lighten her burden, whether it's cooking a meal, cleaning the house, or taking care of the kids. That's kindness. Kindness is wrapped up in consideration and compassion. If she's crying, you don't turn your back on her and walk away, rolling your eyes that she's emotional. You walk over, and you put your arm around her, you ask what's wrong, and if she won't tell you, you either stick it out until she does or just hold her."

The pastor shook his head. "Sometimes women just seem to need to cry. But being kind is showing compassion, showing care and concern. You don't just shrug your shoulders and walk away. If something has happened, if one of her friends has passed away, or her mother is sick in the hospital, you show compassion by lifting her burden so she can go to be with the one that she loves. That doesn't mean that she loves you any less, that means that when it's you in the hospital, when it's you who needs her care, she's going to be with you. That's what that means. So help her. Let her do that. Show your kindness and your care and concern by carrying the burden for her."

"And I think sometimes women get impatient with men, when we act in a way that they think is immature. I'm sorry, but a man is never going to act like a woman. If you want a woman, you won't be sitting here with a man beside you. Don't try to turn him into a woman. You don't want that."

The pastor smiled. "You want his strength, you want his protection, you want his ability to think logically and to shoulder burdens that are heavy. But it comes in a package that sometimes makes loud noises." The pastor raised his brows, and Darby smiled.

"Sometimes he seems like a big kid. Sometimes you shake your head because you feel like he can't be mature about anything. But your definition of mature isn't his. And a lot of times, your definition of responsible isn't his. Although, sometimes men really aren't responsible, but it doesn't matter. Your job is to be kind. Your job is to understand that your way might not be the only way. That what you see might not be what he thinks. And that doesn't make him less, or bad, or wrong, just because he isn't showing the female characteristics you think he should. Be kind to him anyway. Don't insult him, don't tell him he's immature, don't tell him he's irresponsible, don't tell him he's an idiot."

The pastor shifted his hands, taking his Bible and straightening out a page before he continued.

"Kindness helps you build your house. Kindness helps you hold your tongue when maybe you are right, but just because you're right doesn't mean you have to say it. Just because it's 'fact' doesn't mean that the words need to be said. If they aren't kind," he pointed to the Bible, "it says we are not to say them."

He blew out a breath.

"All right, both of you seem like you're paying pretty close attention to what I'm saying. I suppose the one last thing that I want to say is, it says forgiving one another as Christ forgave you."

"Christ forgave you without demanding anything from you. You didn't have to make things up, you didn't have to buy a dozen roses—although it doesn't hurt—or grovel for three days, you don't have to punish anyone by giving them the silent treatment for a week. There is no punishment required, just forgiveness. That's probably one of the hardest things to do. To forgive without demanding payment. But that's how Christ forgave you, so keep that in mind. You don't get to demand payment; God, as the righteous judge, extracts payment. And I have to say that a lot of times I feel like God's punishments are a lot harsher than any punishment I would have handed out."

He looked at both of them. "Do either of you have any questions? Or concerns?"

"I'm good," Jonah said right away. He didn't have any questions, although he appreciated this little counseling session. He had been afraid, but it had actually given him some things to think about.

He hoped that because of the special occasion, he would remember what the pastor said throughout his marriage. Because, like the pastor started out with at the beginning, he wasn't going into this thinking it was going to be a temporary thing. He was going into this thinking that he was going to be married to Darby for the rest of his life. He wanted their marriage to last. These things didn't seem like too onerous of a burden to do in order to have that happen.

"I don't have any questions either," Darby said, her voice low and soft, but it was firm.

He liked that sound. Liked that she wasn't timid or afraid.

"All right, then if you stand with me, over here, I'll go get my wife, and we'll have a witness and we'll get started."

"All right."

Darby and he stood, along with the pastor, who hurried out of the room.

"Are you still good?" Jonah asked as soon as the pastor left.

"Yes."

"Me, too. After I talked to you in your room, I remembered something I had, that I kept, for a long time. It had totally slipped my mind, until just then. I... When my grandmother passed away, my mom gave me her wedding ring. I didn't really know what to do with it, and so I kept it with a few other things I have, a couple of awards from school and a few things from the military.

I grabbed it this morning and put it in my pocket. But we were so busy with getting Amber ready for school and talking to her on the way here, it totally slipped my mind. Do you mind wearing my grandmother's wedding ring?"

Maybe he hadn't needed to say all that and give her a big explanation, but he didn't want her to think that he was just springing it on her at the last moment without considering what she wanted.

"I'd be honored. Will it fit?"

"Would you try it on?"

"Sure," she said, holding out her hand while he dug in his pocket for the ring.

It wasn't a typical wedding band. It had a cluster of three small pearls that were fitted into the band, which was heavy and wide.

A real piece of antique jewelry, although he had no idea of whether it was worth anything.

"It's beautiful," she breathed as he set it in her palm. She looked at it, smiling a little, before she said, "I hadn't even thought about a ring. And this is gorgeous. I... I couldn't have picked out something more beautiful."

"If you want something different, we can grab something, but this will work for the ceremony. Even if it doesn't fit."

She slid it on her finger, where it was slightly loose. "I think we'll need to get it sized, but I'd be honored to wear it."

He smiled, pleased it had worked out. He didn't know what the rest of the day was bringing, or what the rest of their lives would bring, but he did know that he was sure, down to the depths of his soul, that he was making a good decision.

Chapter 17

Darby twisted her ring on her finger, staring at it as the miles flew by.

She was married. In one morning, she had made vows that would affect the rest of her life.

She still wasn't sure she'd wrapped her brain around the enormity of it. But now that the deed was done, her nerves were gone, she still had the peace in her soul, and more than anything, her "let's make a plan to make this work" nature was taking over.

The pastor had provided some wonderful guidance, and she wanted to go and write down her thoughts. She'd do that tonight in bed, but in the meantime, she'd ponder them today.

That passage in Ephesians was so deep and full, and it would be her favorite passage in the Bible, just because the pastor had used it for her wedding. There was so much spiritual wisdom there. Everything a person needed to live a God-honoring, God-fearing, God-pleasing life.

Even sins like coveting and fornication were addressed, although indirectly. After all, if she loved someone, she'd not covet what they had but would be happy for them for having it. And if she was being kind to someone, she wouldn't cause them to defile their body by committing fornication with her.

The pastor obviously hadn't talked about that, but there was so much that was rich and beautiful and practical in that passage that she felt she could think about it for a really long time.

"Regrets?"

Jonah's voice from the other side of the pickup startled her.

"No! No regrets. Just deep thoughts. The pastor had a good message, and I'm glad he insisted on counseling."

"I was thinking the same thing. I don't think I'm going to forget that for a long time. I hope not anyway."

"Me too." She smiled, maybe a little nervous. Their relationship had shifted in a big way, and she still didn't know him very well. She supposed it would be a long time before she felt that way, especially since they wouldn't be spending much time together from now until the end of harvest season.

"I told Gideon I was going to take the day off. Again, with everything else that was going on, I forgot to tell you. I'll...try to do better at keeping you informed."

"I understand. I've been doing a lot of thinking, and the day just seems to be flying by."

"Did you want to do something together?"

"Sure," she said easily, having no idea what he wanted to do.

"What were you planning to do for the rest of the day?"

"I thought I would make brownies, just a little celebration. We didn't have a wedding cake or anything, and I'm not upset about that, but something fun and sweet might be good."

"She said brownies. Amen."

She laughed. "All right, we'll make brownies."

"And anything else you want to do."

"I suppose I should want to do something fun, but I guess I've been seeing those terrible flower beds, and I just kind of wanted to do something about those. Something to make the place a little more welcoming when people come."

"I understand that. So we'll do that too. We'll make brownies, we'll eat brownies, and then, strengthened by our brownies, we'll tackle the flower beds."

"You don't have to do that if you don't want to." She smiled a little, looking across the seat at him.

Surely he had things to do. Things that he wanted to get done, jobs that he didn't want to put off.

"I want to spend time with you. I know I'm not always going to get you, and I have today. So, I want to do whatever you want to do. I just want to be with you."

That...made her feel like he really cared. The same way his determination to make sure that she saw and knew that he thought she was beautiful this morning, that he listened to her concerns and was willing to do whatever they needed to do to shift to make sure that she was on board, and now, he just wanted to spend time with her. Be with her.

He was being romantic, and she would be willing to bet he didn't even know he was.

She wasn't going to point it out though. She was just going to appreciate it. And hope that it was the way he always was and not just the way he was today.

"All right. If you think of something you want to do, I'm in."

"I know. I guess I figured that without even asking you."

"You're just assuming the best of me?" she said with a little laugh.

"Took the pastor's words to heart." He grinned.

But that was true. He had done that automatically before. Just thought the best of her.

She hoped she could do the same for him.

They pulled in and got out, talking a little bit while they were walking up the walk about the things she was thinking for the flower beds.

"We have some manure in the shed. It's been there for years. It's probably nice and decayed and perfect for your beds. Maybe that's one of the things I can do this afternoon."

She appreciated the beautiful sunshiny day. And the fact that he was actually going to help her work on making the house look pretty. Not that he cared. Obviously he'd lived there for several years and hadn't cared whether there were flowers in the beds or not.

It made her smile.

They went in, and she changed her clothes, just put on a T-shirt instead of her button-down, and went into the kitchen.

"Now, I might be a little crazy, but I found this in the pantry. I'm not sure whose it is but thought maybe you'd want to wear it." She held up an apron with a smile.

"That was here when we bought the house, although if you think that I'm going to need it...?"

She pulled her other hand out from behind her back. There had been a frilly pink apron in the pantry and a more manly-looking blue one.

She held the frilly one up in front of him now. "This is the other one I found. I think I'm going to wear it, just for fun. After all, my jeans and T-shirt don't exactly scream frilly pink, but I think it'll be fun."

She shrugged and threw the blue apron over the back of one of the chairs.

"I was just kidding about you."

He reached over and grabbed it. "I'll wear it to match you. This does not affect my manhood at all."

She laughed, raising her brows in a bit of a challenge. "Lots of men wear aprons. That is not a test of your manhood." She put the pink one over her head.

"Really? Actually, I think you look pretty good in it. It's very formfitting, and this will make me look fat."

"I think you're making fun of someone, but I'm not sure who," she said as she wrapped the strings around her waist, reaching back to tie them.

"I'll get that," he said, taking the strings from her hand. She let them go. Smiling.

That had not been her plan with the aprons, but maybe it would work out okay.

"I'm not insulting anyone, just making fun of women in general, I think."

"And our tendency to be concerned about how we look?"

"You put an awful lot of store on that, and while I suppose that men really are visually driven, I guess I've lived long enough that I'm more concerned about having someone who is kind, fun, who can laugh at herself—and me—and will roll with things than I am about what size pants she wears."

"I'm happy to hear that," she said. "I think."

"You are. Because with all the things that have been happening lately, you've reacted with grace every time, and I've been admiring you."

"Thank you. But you've been very considerate of me, more considerate than I deserve. It's been easy to react the way I know I'm supposed to, when I know that you're going to make sure that I'm taken care of."

"I think the Lord might have been onto something there, because when someone is nice to you, it makes you want to be nice back to them, and then you want to do more nice things for them, which makes them want to do more nice things for you, and it's like an upward spiral."

"The opposite is probably true. Where, if someone's unkind to you, your tendency is to do something unkind back, and then you continue to do unkind things to each other, to get each other back, when if you would just allow that to slide, there would be no downward spiral."

"Amazing the way the Bible is what a lot of people consider an archaic book but has so much wisdom that applies across the board for today."

"That's because it was written by the One who made us. It's our handbook."

They smiled at each other, and she realized his hands had lingered at her waist.

He should have had her apron tied a long time ago, but they'd been talking, and he hadn't moved. His hands just rested on the small of her back, where he tied her apron, not too tight. His fingers resting there. She could feel each spot.

"I wanted to thank you," he said into the stillness of the kitchen.

"For what?" she asked in surprise.

"For taking a chance on me."

"You took the same chance on me."

"I didn't seek you out. I didn't even know about you. You're the one who thought it might be a good idea to make sure that Amber's dad, who didn't know about his daughter, had had a say in her life. Then, you kind of got blindsided with a whole bunch of different things, and...thank you."

Her throat felt tight, and she had trouble swallowing.

Time would tell whether they'd made the right decision or not. She was confident they could make it work, confident he was a man she could learn to trust and love.

She hoped she was the kind of woman with whom he could do the same.

Chapter 18

Jonah's hands dropped, and he stepped back. "Where do we start?"

She appreciated him doing that. She wasn't sure how to handle all the emotion she was feeling. Didn't want to go too fast in any direction. So she shook it off and focused on what they were planning.

"We need flour and sugar, cocoa, and baking powder. I checked before we left today, to make sure you had all of those things in the pantry. I was a little surprised that you had cocoa."

He laughed. "Gideon has tried his hand over the years at cooking, especially during the winter. He's tried various things, to various degrees of success, or maybe I should say various degrees of failure, but regardless, that was something he got when he had an idea about making a red velvet cake. Apparently, red velvet is actually code for chocolate and an excuse to use a lot of cream cheese. Which I did not know until Gideon attempted it."

"I think it takes a lot of red food coloring."

"Yeah. But the cream cheese icing was good."

"I love cream cheese icing." They exchanged a glance, and she got the impression that he was a big fan of it too.

She got the flour down and scooped some out while she pointed to the sugar and instructed him on how much to put in the bowl.

"So you talked about Gideon experimenting in the kitchen. But you didn't?"

"We all took turns cooking, and some of us were better at it than others. I was one of the others."

"Really? I would think you'd be really good."

"I suppose if I actually looked up some recipes and tried to follow them, I might be better, but my idea of cooking was making hamburgers. And if I was getting really wild and crazy, I'd cook hot dogs too."

"You can cook hamburgers?"

"Sure can. We even have a grill out back, and I can do them pretty well on there."

"It's just something in a man's DNA that enables him to do grilling well."

"It's all in the way you click the tongs together."

She laughed. "That's totally necessary."

"Hey, don't question the procedures of the master griller."

"Well, I have to admit that my catering business didn't include much grilling. I have an aversion to working over an open flame."

"Does that aversion have any grounding in actual experience?"

"Well, when I was younger, I did catch our house on fire once."

"Oh, she says it so casually now, after I've already married her and it's too late for me to change my mind."

She laughed as they mixed the dry ingredients together. "Well, if it eases your mind any, I haven't repeated it."

"In other words, in your lifetime, you've only caught one house on fire? That still sounds like a sketchy track record to me."

"You've never caught anything on fire?"

"I caught my beard on fire once. That's why I typically keep it cut pretty close."

"Your beard?" she asked, laughing.

"Yeah. I used to keep it a lot longer. I had let it grow out for a year or so, and it was down to here." He put a hand in the middle of his chest.

"Wow. It's hard for me to picture you with a beard like that."

"After I got out of the military. They had made us keep our hair so short, I guess I kind of rebelled a little."

"I'll say."

"Anyway, we were at a restaurant, celebrating Gideon's birthday, and they brought out like a cupcake with a candle in it?"

"I've seen those."

"And the waitress passed it across me to Gideon. While I was passing it, I leaned forward. I don't even know why. I don't know if I was just adjusting my seat or whatever, but I was laughing at something someone else said, passing the cupcake, leaning forward, and I was not paying attention. The cupcake candle went under my beard and caught it on fire."

"So you don't look like you have scars on your face, but come to think of it, I've never really seen you completely clean-shaven."

"It's a little warmer in North Dakota if you keep something covering your face, but no. Gideon has really fast reflexes, which I appreciate. They're almost as quick as his sense of humor."

"He is funny," Darby said. "If you like that type of humor." She added that last bit, not wanting Jonah to think she admired Gideon over him.

"Anyway, he grabbed his glass of soda and threw it in my face. It's the one time someone's done that to me that I really appreciated it. Put the fire right out."

"Wow. That is quick thinking. I guess you're kind of ingrained to not do that to someone, I would almost try to pat it out and totally forget I had a glass of liquid sitting right beside me that would help."

"Yeah. I would say I was glad that that's the way most people think, because none of the other guys at the table, there were six other ones, thought to do that right away. But once Gideon did it, it's like he unleashed a torrent, and I practically drowned with everyone else throwing their drinks on me."

"Oh. That doesn't sound good."

"No. It was wet and cold and sticky. But we were almost done eating. That was dessert. So it was a good birthday for the most part, and I went home, took a shower, and everything was okay."

"All right. If you say so. I think I would have been a little annoyed at the people who threw their drinks on me after the fire was already out."

"They said they thought it was smoldering and they didn't want it to flame up again. But there's just something really deeply satisfying about throwing a glass of liquid on someone and having a really good excuse to do so. You know?"

She laughed. "If you say so."

"Maybe it's a man thing, but I think they just had fun with it. And it didn't bother me at all."

She liked that about him. That he could end up with lots of glasses of drinks on him and just shrug it off with a laugh.

She didn't think that she would be quite so easygoing.

They cracked eggs and added that to the butter and sugar mixture.

He had sifted the flour and cocoa together, and they poured that in.

"These are simple, but brownie batter is probably my favorite batter of anything, except for maybe angel food cake."

"I have never attempted to make an angel food cake. And I don't envision that attempt happening at any time in my future either."

"Oh? We're not going to do that after we come in from working on the flower beds?"

He paused, looking up at her, maybe trying to determine whether or not she was joking or serious. "You want to?"

"I'm teasing. Angel food cake is not a cake for beginners. I made a lot of them before I got any good at it."

"I like to eat them, but I think I like brownies better."

They poured the batter in the pan and then stuck it in the oven.

JUST A COWBOY'S SECRET BABY

"We need to come back in thirty minutes and check on that. But in the meantime, we can clean up here and head outside if you want to?" she said, not wanting to push him if he wasn't serious about wanting to help her with her flowers.

But he had been, and they went out and got started, pausing to take the brownies out of the oven and then pausing again in another half an hour to go eat some.

They sat on the swing, eating and talking and making plans. Plans for the yard, the garden and the flowers, and getting chicks, which she was really excited about. "I might even be more excited than Amber is about the chicks."

"We'll have to get them from the feed store. I like supporting our local businesses. But if you have a certain kind you want, and they're not available locally, we can order them online. Sometimes you have to wait a while, but there are a lot of varieties you can choose from."

"Varieties? You mean there are different breeds of chickens?" she asked with a lifted brow. Who knew? Actually, it made sense that there would be, but she just had never thought about it. Like people do that and keep track of them.

"Oh, man, yes. There are birds that are bred specifically for meat, and there are birds bred specifically for eggs. Then there's some birds that, believe it or not, are bred specifically for the feathers they produce, because they make fishing lures out of them."

"Wow. That sounds like quite a business."

"I suppose it is. Like anything else. But if there's a demand for it, someone's going to step in and figure out a way to make money off it."

"And that is the way it should be. After all, if you have the gumption to get up and do the work to fill a demand, you deserve to make money from it."

"I agree with you completely. It's nuts to think that anything would happen if people weren't rewarded for their work. Maybe in an ideal society where everyone was Christians, and everyone was looking out after the other person, but that's not the way our society is today. Everyone looks out for themselves. A society based on people doing things out of the goodness of their heart really isn't possible without goodness and virtue underlying everything."

"I agree with that completely. After all, I started my own catering business, and I would have been pretty upset if I hadn't been able to profit off all the hard work I put into it when I was getting it off the ground."

"That's why I was planning on working so hard this summer. You don't start a business without putting a lot of sweat and blood and tears into it. There are a lot of ups and downs, a lot of crazy pitfalls along the way, things you hadn't anticipated, and things that go terribly wrong. You wouldn't want to put all the work into doing something and then watch someone else take the money you earned and use it for themselves, when they haven't lifted a finger."

"Of course not."

"Talking of work, you ready to get back on it?" he asked.

"Sure. Give me your plate. I'll take these in, and we'll get started again. I'm surprised how much we got done. I really thought this would take a long time."

"If we work hard, we might get done by late afternoon. I'm not sure what time the bus comes by, but Amber can help us if she wants to. Unless you want to quit when she gets home."

"It will be good for her to do something other than play the piano and schoolwork. Although, we could take a little break when she gets here, give her a brownie, and talk about her day. I'm really hoping it went well."

"Me too."

"And I hope our decision to not tell her that we were getting married until after we did it was the right one."

"I think in a perfect world, we would have told her before, but I think we were right to not want to upset her before she started a new school in a new state with completely new people."

She nodded and took their plates inside.

She hoped they were right. She thought they were. She actually thought that Amber might be happy. Not that Amber had ever expressed much of a desire to have a dad. She certainly asked about one over the years, and they'd talked about whether or not she would ever get one. But Amber hadn't seemed upset that was missing in her life.

It had been Darby's concern when she adopted her as a single mom.

But being raised by a single mom was better than being aborted, so she felt like it was at least half of a win.

Amber didn't typically have a lot of drama, and she didn't anticipate there being any problems.

But if there was one thing that she had learned as a mom over the years, it was that normally it was when she didn't anticipate problems that she had the biggest ones.

That was what had her the most worried.

Putting the dishes in the sink and making sure the brownies were covered and set back, she walked outside, hoping that when her daughter returned home from school, they would have a productive conversation that ended on a positive note.

She also said a short prayer that Amber had had a great day of school and that her transition into her new classroom went smoothly.

Chapter 19

"Wow. I can't believe how much we've accomplished in an afternoon," Darby said. She put her hands on her legs as she knelt down in front of the last flower bed.

There were several beds in the front of the house, several more behind, and one running along each side.

They'd managed to get all of the weeds out of them and had moved manure from the old chicken coop into the beds, as well as gotten the borders fixed up and straightened.

There weren't any flowers in them, but Jonah had said that it might be a bit early to try to plant anything that wasn't cold hardy.

Eventually she wanted to put perennials in them, but she would be happy with some annuals this year.

The school bus rumbled in the distance, and she looked up.

"Wow. Perfect timing."

"I'm ready for another snack of brownies."

"You are. You've been working hard. I would never have gotten all this work done if it weren't for you. Actually, I probably wouldn't have wanted to put manure on them at all if it weren't for you."

"Trust me, you'll appreciate the fact that it's there when your flowers do a lot better."

"I'm trusting you, because to me, that stuff was junk."

And boy, did it smell. She had never smelled anything that terrible in her life, and she felt like she was probably going to end up with some kind of dread disease, but Jonah had assured her that chicken manure was not only not going to hurt her, but it would make her flowers grow.

Then, almost as an aside, he said if there was any mouse dirt in it, it can really mess a person up.

She wanted to flip out about the whole mouse thing. She didn't want mice anywhere. She certainly didn't want mouse dirt anywhere either. But she supposed that was one of the things that she was going to have to deal with since she was now living in the country, and especially since they were living in an old house.

He promised that if she ever saw a mouse, he'd kill it for her.

If he was home.

As much fun as she had with him that day, as much as she enjoyed working with him, the idea of him leaving was getting harder and harder to handle.

She'd been alone for forever, so it didn't make any sense that she would be dreading her husband leaving. Especially after just a couple days together. But it was the truth.

Maybe it was the idea of being alone where there were no houses in sight. She certainly wasn't used to living in such a remote area, but she knew that was the way North Dakota was.

She liked Jonah. Really liked him. Enjoyed his sense of humor, his ability to tell stories, his work ethic, and his commonsense approach to life.

She liked that there was someone she could lean on, and depend on, and count on.

And she really liked that there was someone else who wanted the very best for Amber. The same as she did.

The bus drew to a stop, and her little girl walked off.

She could tell immediately from the way Amber was walking, the spring in her step, and the glow on her face, that it had been a good day.

"I'm pretty sure we're going to hear good news," she murmured as she straightened, brushing her knees off and dusting her hands.

"That's good. We still on board to talk to her about everything?"

"I think so. I think we need to talk to her and make sure, but from the way she's looking, I think we're going to hear some really good news."

"I love that you can tell that just by looking at her."

"You'll be able to, too. When you get to know someone, you can just tell, you know?"

"I guess. I suppose if I walk into a room with one glance at Gideon, I know whether he's going to be joking or whether it's going to be one of those rare occasions where I'm better off just walking on by."

"Yeah. That's what I'm talking about." She grinned up at him, figuring he would know.

"I'm just glad to know it's not some mystical bond between mother and daughter, something that I'm going to be left out of."

"I'm not going to leave you out of anything, if I can help it," she said and hoped that was completely true. She didn't want it to be her fighting him and him trying to push to be included and her not allowing it.

She hoped there was never a time that happened.

"Hey, kiddo," she said as Amber got closer. She and Jonah walked to the end of the walk to meet her. "How was your day?"

"Oh, Mommy, you wouldn't believe what happened today!" Amber said, skipping a little, her backpack bouncing on her back.

It always pulled at Darby's heartstrings just a little, to see her daughter coming back from being gone all day. She always felt it was crazy that she sent her child away from her all day. It was kind of hard to wrap her mind around the idea that was what everyone did. And it was perfectly okay.

"What happened?" she asked, thinking that she could say the exact same thing back to Amber. That Amber wouldn't believe what happened to her today.

"The teacher took me up to the front of the class and introduced me, and asked who wanted to sit beside me, and everybody raised their hand," Amber said, her voice holding happiness and joy. "So then the teacher said that I could get to choose who I wanted to sit beside. And since Merritt was in my class, and I knew her, I went and sat beside her. So, I had a friend right away."

"That's great."

"And then we had music class, and the music teacher didn't know me, so she took me aside and asked me my name and everything, and I told her, and she asked if I played any instruments. So, I got to play the piano in music class."

"Wow. That made you feel right at home."

"Yep."

"Would you like to sit on the porch and have some brownies?" Darby asked.

"I'm tired of sitting. I want to run around a little bit. We didn't have a garden like this in Baltimore. And it just makes you want to run!" Amber said, shrugging out of her backpack as they reached the steps.

"That'll be fine. If you want to run around after you change your clothes, you can."

"Can I have brownies afterward?" Amber asked, looking at her mom as she opened the door.

"You sure can."

Chapter 20

They went inside, and Jonah watched them disappear.

He could stay out. It had been quite a day.

The wedding, working with Darby, the anticipation of telling his daughter that he was her father. And of course, the marriage counseling.

Maybe that had brought everything home to him, that he was pledging his life to be responsible for two other human beings.

And there might be more.

That set his stomach rolling. The very idea.

Remembering that they had a soccer ball and a volleyball from when they moved in, he walked out to the shed, digging them up easily.

Finding the air pump, he topped both of them off, although they held air surprisingly well.

She might not want to kick a ball around, but he figured she wouldn't realize it was an option unless he offered it to her.

On the one hand, he wished that they could have just told her and gotten it over with. On the other, he figured it was good for her to wait to unwind from school and then to spend a little bit more time together.

He was glad he'd made the effort to walk over and get the balls, because as he was coming back to the house, Amber came out and her eyes lit up when she saw balls he carried.

"A soccer ball! Will you play with me?"

"I was kind of hoping we could," he said, wishing he had changed into his sneakers too.

But he'd done plenty of things in his cowboy boots, and he figured playing soccer would just be one more.

He hadn't bet on the blisters he would have by the time they were done playing forty-five minutes later.

His feet hurt to walk, but he was trying hard not to limp, because he really didn't want to quit. Even though he knew they had things to talk about, playing games was a good way to get to know someone.

Even Darby had joined in, and it was a great family time. They didn't keep score, but they still laughed and had fun together. And that was the idea behind it, the personal interaction, the full body movement, and the idea that they were building relationships as a family.

He wasn't very good at it, but it was important that his family be strong, and if that meant he had to get good at things that he normally wasn't, then that's what he'd do.

Ten minutes later, Darby had served them all brownies, and they sat on the porch steps, holding plates and with big glasses of water beside them.

It had been a beautiful day, and he was sure he would remember it for the rest of his life. Perfect weather, and everything had gone well.

Up until this point.

He wasn't sure why he was so anxious about Amber's reaction, but he was.

"We have something we wanted to tell you, Amber," Darby began. But she didn't get to say any more, because they heard a car motor and looked over at the driveway.

A car slowly came into sight, motoring toward them. It was a sedan, not a late model, not one that Jonah recognized.

He was immediately on guard, just because he was with his family, and he didn't want anything to happen to them.

Normally, he wouldn't worry at all about a stranger coming in. Although they were far enough back out of the way that people didn't just wander in.

"Maybe someone wants to talk about crop dusting and didn't want to call," he murmured.

But the car didn't go toward the shed. It came toward the house.

Maybe because that's where they were all sitting.

Jonah stood. The driver was a woman.

It most likely was not going to be someone about crop dusting, although that was still a possibility.

"Oh, my goodness, Jonah. That's Nora."

It stood to reason that Darby recognized her before he did. He hadn't seen her in nine years, except for the two pictures Darby had showed him.

Her hand had gone to her chest, and her words were whispered, laced with fear.

He moved over, putting his arm around her shoulders and pulling her close to him.

She came easily.

"Miss Nora? The lady who used to come over to our house sometimes in Baltimore?" Amber said, peering at the car, brownie crumbs sticking to the side of her mouth.

"Yes." Her word held dread.

"It's okay." He wanted to say more, but he didn't want to upset Amber or bring attention to the fact that Darby seemed upset, since Amber seemed oblivious.

"She's moving to North Dakota too?" she asked, after she had swallowed her brownie.

"I don't know. I haven't talked to her."

"Do you want me to go over? I can send her away?" Jonah put his mouth right by Darby's ear.

She took a deep breath, as though steeling herself, and he wished there was more he could do.

Finally she lifted her head so her face was beside his ear.

"My lawyer advised me that there was nothing she could do. I blocked her phone calls and text messages the last time she threatened to take me to court for custody of Amber. I... I didn't know this was going to happen."

"It's okay. We'll deal." Whatever it was, whatever she wanted, they'd figure out.

"Of course. And no. Don't send her away. Amber has already recognized her, and we don't send people away for no good reason. I didn't want this, but I guess it's going to play out however it does."

"And we'll go through this together. Okay?"

He wanted to know that she was on his side. On his team. They were standing shoulder to shoulder against whatever happened. And as long as he knew that, he could fight for whatever they needed to fight for.

"Of course. Always." She looked at him and smiled. His lips turned up too.

There was no humor, just shared companionship. They knew they were together, and whatever happened, they would stand beside each other. That's what he wanted.

By that time, Nora had parked and gotten out of her car.

She stood beside it, shading her eyes from the setting sun.

"Darby Woods," Nora said. And then she got a big smile on her face and spread her arms wide. "And, Amber, my precious darling," she said, running down the walk with her arms spread, charging toward Amber, who shrank back a little.

"Mommy?" Amber said uncertainly.

"It's okay. If you don't want to hug someone, you don't have to."

"All right," Amber said. At that, Jonah decided he was going to take a step down and step in front of his wife and daughter.

Chapter 21

"Hello, Nora," he said, with a hand stretched out, stopping her mid flight up the stairs, since she couldn't get to Amber with him standing in front of her.

"It's been a long time," he said, his hand still held out, offering her the opportunity to shake it.

"Jonah?" she asked, her eyes wide.

Maybe she hadn't recognized him at first, with the stubble on his face and his hair an inch longer than it had been when he'd been in the service.

"It's me."

"You witch," Nora said, venom dripping from her tone as she peered around Jonah's shoulder, looking at Darby.

"I'd appreciate it if you don't talk to my wife like that," he said, hating that Darby had to hear that.

She was already doing the best she could and feeling like it wasn't enough. She didn't need someone coming in and tearing her down, calling her names.

"You came in here and got your fingers on him before I could say anything. When I told you about him, and told you that he was honorable and upright, and that I wanted to reconcile, I should have known that you were going to come out here and try to step in front of me." She rolled her eyes. "She's probably told you a pile of lies about me. But I promise you nothing is true. I've been fighting her for years trying to get her to do the best thing for my precious daughter, and she refuses."

Her eyes blinked, while Darby gasped, and he thought she was going to say something, refute the charges, but she didn't.

Was it true? Had Nora really talked to Darby before they left, telling her about him? Had they known for years? Her story wasn't lining up with Darby's, just pieces of it. And Jonah wasn't sure what to believe, until he remembered.

Darby had never lied to him. Not at all. And Nora had lied over and over.

"Why didn't you tell me you were pregnant when you left me?" he asked.

"I was young," Nora said, after a small pause, which he assumed she used trying to think up an excuse that would sound believable to him and also be something to gain his sympathy. "You know I was young. We both were. Neither one of us should have gotten married."

He disagreed. It didn't matter what their age was. They were fine getting married, as long as they made the choice to keep their vows. Age was not an indicator of character. It could be an indicator of wisdom, although not always.

"Did you want something?" he asked.

"I want to see my daughter. After all, I gave birth to her." She sounded a little dramatic, and Jonah had to work not to roll his eyes.

Like giving birth to her was the only thing that mattered.

"You haven't raised her, and she's not your child. Darby is her mother."

"Amber doesn't know. Amber doesn't know that I'm actually her mommy," Nora said, her voice raising on the last word as she tried to look around Jonah's other shoulder, to meet the eyes of her daughter.

"You wanted to kill her. And you would have if it hadn't been for Darby." Everything Darby said would be true. He was banking on it. "And Darby has sacrificed everything in order to raise her right. I'm sorry, you gave up your rights to her—"

"You don't understand what she's trying to do." She pointed a finger at Amber. "That little girl has talent that the world should see. Everyone should hear the way she plays. They should have access to that, and the world should know. Amber deserves to have her place on the stage, to have the adulation of millions, to be celebrated for the true prodigy that she is. Talent like hers only comes around once every several hundred years. Do you realize what a special child Amber is?"

"I realize she is a child," Jonah said evenly, cringing inside. He didn't know how this was affecting Amber. He wanted to take a hold of Nora and throw her off his property. There was already going to be a lot of explaining to do. And all because of Nora not caring to keep her mouth shut.

"Amber, I think we need to go inside," Darby said, her voice low and soothing.

"Mommy? Are you not my mommy?"

"No! She's not," Nora practically shouted.

"Amber. Darby is your mom. Go inside with her while I handle things."

He hadn't given Amber any specific commands since he met her. That was the first one, and she obeyed without question.

He'd have to thank her later.

After they disappeared, he crossed his arms over his chest and looked down at Nora's red and mottled face.

He almost expected her to strike him, she looked so angry. Her fists were clenched at her sides.

"How dare you try to keep her from me! You're listening to Darby's lies. I did nothing but try to do the very best for Amber

152

that I could, and she's done nothing but try to hide her from the rest of the world, keeping her to herself."

"Where's the benefit in that?" Jonah asked casually.

"Well... Of course... I know..." Nora sputtered.

"It's okay. I'll wait," Jonah said, his anger boiling in his chest, but his demeanor was calm and serene.

God loved Nora too. As angry as he was with her. As much as he wanted to throttle her for what she had done to his daughter, this was a person who needed the Lord. Just as much as he did.

"Do you realize how much she's worth?" Nora finally said.

"She's worth more than money to me," Jonah said, nodding his head. "I would've wanted to know about her, Nora. I would've wanted to know my daughter. I can't believe you walked off and never told me."

"You are a joke. You were never around. You left me alone all the time. I didn't want to be a single mom raising your kid by myself."

"Is that really it?" he asked, knowing that he had been gone a lot, but not all the time.

He'd been deployed once, for sixteen months, and it had been a tough time, but that was the only time he had left her. Otherwise, he was gone as much as a normal working man. It wasn't like he went out and partied with his friends on the weekend or even went out for drinks after work. He did what he had to do and came home to his wife. She was the one who wasn't normally home.

Of course, she claimed she was working, but he wasn't sure that was entirely true. He had believed her at the time, but he'd never seen any money from a job and had never dug into it.

"I deserve part of the money that kid makes! I went through the pain of childbirth. I went through the anguish of pregnancy. It was terrible. And you were nowhere around."

"Because you left me," Jonah said, irritated. He could hardly be blamed for not being around if she had walked out on him. But he was even more irritated that Nora was showing her hand and seeing dollar signs when she saw Amber. "And I really don't like talking about my daughter like she has some kind of monetary value, and that's all you see."

"Of course not! I want the best for Amber too. If you had a talent like that, wouldn't you want the world to know it? Wouldn't you want the adulation of millions of people all over the world? Wouldn't you want to be onstage in New York City, the lights and the crowds and the cheering and everyone thinking you're amazing and talented and worshipping you?"

"No. Actually, I wouldn't."

"But Amber does! She wants everyone to hear her play. She wants to be on that stage. She wants that career. And every second she's not practicing, every second she's not taking lessons, every second she's not working to build a following is working against her. Anyone can play the piano when they're twenty-five. But an eight-year-old? She needs to jump on this now while her earning potential is the highest. Don't you see that, Jonah?"

"No. I don't."

What he could see was that Nora walking out on him was the very best thing that could possibly have happened. Not just for him, but for Amber too. That God had His hand on Amber, when Nora met Darby and Darby talked her into not aborting the baby. He could see that God had brought Darby into Amber's life, knowing Darby would be willing to make the sacrifices necessary to raise her the way she needed to be raised.

"When I was a kid, I wanted to be a kid. I wanted to play. I wanted to kick the ball around my yard and eat brownies on the front porch. I wanted to lie on the grass and look up at the sky and dream. I didn't want to be stuck in a room forced to practice for hours on end so that I could be paraded around like a pet monkey at a zoo."

"That's because you have no imagination. You have no inspiration. You have no drive to be the best you can be. You're lacking in all those areas, that's why Amber needs me. I can see the big picture. I can tell what she needs. I can be the person that Amber needs in order to take her to the top. And that's just right, since I am her mother."

"Is your name on her birth certificate?"

"I'm working on that," Nora said, her eyes shooting daggers, her jaw set.

"Well, the birth certificate that I see has Darby's name on it. And if it's okay with Darby, I'll be having custody of her as well, since I'm the father. And I'm sure it will be interesting to a judge to know that you not only didn't tell me about our daughter, even though we were married, but that you were looking to get an abortion. It is only by the grace of God that you weren't successful."

"You don't know how miserable being pregnant is," Nora muttered.

"I guess sometimes we have to live through misery, making a personal sacrifice, for the good of someone else."

"I did. I had her. And that was painful as well. Extremely painful, excruciatingly painful. And you weren't there."

"I would've been. And you know it. You made that choice, Nora. Now you need to live with it."

"This won't be the last of this."

"Maybe not. But I guess we'll just do the best we can, fighting as hard as possible, to try to do the right thing for Amber. And the right thing for Amber is for her to never see you again. So please don't come back. If you do, I'll have to report you to the police for trespassing."

"You wouldn't."

Jonah raised a brow. Oh yes, he would. It was all he could do not to pull his phone out of his pocket and do it now.

"You haven't seen the last of me," Nora said through clenched teeth as she turned around and stomped back down the stairs.

Jonah didn't move, not until she'd turned around, spinning her tires as she did so, and wheeled out the driveway.

He wasn't sure what exactly she was going to do, but he wasn't going to allow himself to worry about it. He might contact a lawyer, just to make sure their bases were covered, but from what Darby had said, Nora didn't have a legal leg to stand on. She was just out trying to ruffle and upset them. And he wasn't going to allow it.

Taking a breath, he turned and walked into the house.

Chapter 22

Darby stood in the living room, looking out the window. She couldn't keep herself from giving a sigh of relief as Nora stomped down the steps and drove away.

That didn't mean the threat was completely over, but it did mean that their little family was safe for the time being.

She could hear voices through the closed door, but she couldn't understand everything they had said.

As long as Jonah didn't believe Nora's lies, they'd be fine.

She had to trust that Jonah would believe her, even though he hadn't known her that long. But she'd never lied to him. She'd been straight with him from the beginning. Hopefully, that counted for something.

She hurried to the door, opening it, as he turned and pulled the screen door open.

"She's gone," he said, smiling a little, but his face still looked pinched.

"You're upset," she said, knowing it was a stupid thing to say. Of course he was upset. But she didn't know what else to say.

"I'm not angry. Frustrated, but not worrying. And I tried to remind myself that Nora is a human being too, and God loves her."

"Good thought," she said, smiling.

"Is Amber okay?"

"Yeah. She was sitting at the table, and I allowed her to color and eat brownies. I told her that you and I will explain everything to her as soon as Nora was gone."

"I guess that's now."

"Yeah. I guess so. Anything I need to know?" she asked softly, glancing into the kitchen where Amber focused intently on the coloring in front of her. Art was something she loved almost as much as she loved playing the piano.

"No. Just you were right. She was about the money. And the fame and popularity, and she feels the time is ticking because once Amber is old enough to actually have a career like a normal person, she won't be sought after, because, according to her, anyone can be a pianist at twenty-five, it's the fact that she's a child that makes her interesting."

"I just hope you didn't believe her that we had talked about you. I promise, I looked you up myself."

He came closer to her, putting his hand on her arm and putting the other one around her neck, bending down low, and saying, "I believe you. I do. I admit, when she was saying things rapid fire and so confidently, it made me waver for just a second, until I got my footing. Not more than a second, I promise. Because Nora hadn't been honest with me when we were married, and you have never lied. Of course I'm going to believe you."

Her soul breathed a sigh of relief. "Good to know."

She felt like a hundred ton of bricks had been lifted from her chest, and she also felt like whatever they had to face, it would be okay, now that she knew for sure he believed her.

Of course, there was also the concern that Amber would be negatively affected by everything.

She liked where his hand was, liked the strength she felt when he touched her, liked the reassurance as well, but she needed to move away. They needed to make sure her daughter was okay. She wanted to get things straightened out so their world could be peaceful once more.

"This is not how I had pictured things going," she mumbled as she moved, turning toward the kitchen.

"Does life usually turn out the way we think it's going to?"

"Not usually, but sometimes we can work really hard and accomplish things we never thought possible."

"That's true, but we can't usually change people."

"I think you're saying that Nora is going to be a thorn in our sides for a long time."

"I think she will be. But I also don't think she's going to win. First of all, your adoption was legal, and there is no reason for a court to overturn it. Second of all, we are on the Lord's side. And that really is more important than anything else."

"You're right. Whatever He allows in our lives, it's just to see how we're going to react, if we're going to trust Him, and if we're going to grow."

"That's right."

They moved into the kitchen, and Amber looked up immediately, putting her crayon down, her eyes big.

"Did Miss Nora leave?" she asked.

"She did, honey," Jonah said, going around and pulling the chair out from the end of the table while Darby went around and sat down next to Amber.

"Why did she say you weren't my mom?" Amber said softly. "And that she was?"

"She said that because she gave you up for adoption before you were even born. I said I would adopt you, and I went to all of your appointments, with Nora, knowing that once you were born, you were going to be mine."

"So she's my...birth mother?"

"Yes." It made sense that Amber would know the term. Not just because she was intelligent, but because it was something that wasn't completely unusual anymore.

"I wondered why she told me you weren't my mom back in Baltimore."

"She did?" Darby said, her eyes going wide, her spine straightening.

"Relax, Mom. I didn't believe her. She told me that you weren't my mom. And I knew you wouldn't lie to me. So I shrugged and acted like I didn't care. Because I don't."

"Why didn't you tell me?"

"Because I didn't want you to be upset. Every time Miss Nora came, it upset you, and I knew it had to do with me playing the piano and her wanting me to do things that you didn't want me to do. And she made me uncomfortable. Even without her upsetting you. Just something in the way she looked at me. I don't want her to be my mom. I want you."

"For all intents and purposes, I am. I didn't give birth to you, but I chose you. I wanted you, and...she was willing to give you up."

Darby wasn't sure how much more to say. This wasn't the way she intended this conversation to go either. This day had been full of surprises. Good ones, bad ones, but God had been working them all out. She believed that.

Her eyes met Jonah's, and a question went across the table.

He nodded.

"There's a reason I came to Sweet Water, and there is a reason that I met Jonah."

"She said he's my dad?" Amber asked, her finger playing with one of the crayons, like that had been a question that had been bothering her.

"Yes. Nora and Jonah were married, and when Nora got pregnant, she left Jonah without telling him. She was...going to get an abortion, but I talked her out of it and said I wanted to adopt you. Jonah didn't know about you. Not until I came to North Dakota. And part of the reason I came was because I wanted you to know your dad, and I knew he would want to know you. Because you're pretty awesome." She smiled, trying to let all the love she had for Amber show in her eyes.

Amber grinned a little, but then she looked uncomfortably at Jonah. "Do you like me?"

His mouth opened in surprise, like that was not the question he was expecting. "I do. I like you a lot. In fact, I love you. I love you just because you're my daughter."

Darby was so proud of Jonah. Those might not have been easy words to say, because he couldn't know how Amber was going to react to them. She might not want a father. She didn't look totally thrilled, and Darby wasn't sure what to do about that.

Amber said, "Really?"

"Really. I...hope eventually you'll like me too."

"Can I call you Dad?"

A muscle twitched in Jonah's jaw. "Yeah. I'd like that."

"Do I have to?"

"No. Not all," Jonah said immediately.

Darby's hands clenched. She prayed that Amber would want to. That she would tell him. That she would give him some sign that she appreciated the lengths he'd gone to to try to make her a part of his life and to protect her to the best of his ability.

"I think I want to. I... I always wanted a dad, but I never wanted to make Mom feel bad."

"Amber," Darby said, surprised.

"Well, it's true. I mean, other kids don't have dads, or they have two dads, and I just wanted to be normal. You know? I wanted to have a mom and a dad and me. I don't know why. That's just what I wanted," she said, picking up the paper she'd been coloring on.

"I think that's a natural thing. That's what I'd like our family to be, a mom and a dad and you. Which kind of brings me to the other thing that I had to tell you."

"Mom, really? Don't you think this is enough for one day?" Amber said, sounding like a little adult.

"I hope this will be a good announcement," she said, hoping that her voice held that emotion. She wasn't sure that it did. "I did something today with Jonah, and we wanted to talk to you about it before we did it, but we didn't want to upset you before you went to school."

"You don't need to worry about that. School was good."

"I know. Which is why we decided that we could tell you now. Although, we think this is going to be happy news for you."

"All right," Amber said, putting the crayon down and crossing her arms over her chest. "Hit me."

Darby laughed and rolled her eyes. Then her gaze caught on Jonah's, and he was smiling too. "Jonah and I got married this morning."

"You what?" Amber asked, her eyes opening wide, flying from Darby to Jonah and back to Darby. "You got married without me?"

"We did."

"I can't believe it. You got married without me, which was not cool, but I went to school with just a mom, and I came home, and now I have a mom and dad?"

"That's right. Your mom married your dad, and now you have both."

"Wow. I can't believe it. If I would've known this was going to happen when we moved to North Dakota, I wouldn't have been so sad about leaving Baltimore."

"So it's a good thing?" Darby couldn't help but ask, just wanting to confirm it.

"Yes! I can't believe it!" She had a big smile on her face, and then she pushed back her chair. "Aren't you guys gonna hug me?" she asked, and Jonah and Darby laughed. Then they both jumped up, coming around the table and hugging their daughter between them.

It was a moment that Darby was sure she would remember for the rest of her life. Their first family hug.

Chapter 23

E llen used a pocketknife to slice an apple, giving the High-
lander heifer she stood beside one piece at a time.

Her uncle Tadgh was talking to a buyer, and several more potential buyers had strolled over.

Her heifer, Cheerio, happily munched at the apple, calmly ignoring the chaos around her.

A group of teen girls had picked up a hose not far away, and
squealed as they squirted each other with it.

Stuff like that usually wasn't tolerated at the sale barn, not on sale
nights. But it was a Tuesday afternoon, and the girls had been out
jogging together in a group. They'd stopped at the sale barn on
their way back into town to get cooled off, apparently.

At least that's what it looked like to Ellen. They were all older
than her, although she recognized them from school, but they
weren't in her grade.

It looked like the cheerleading team, led by the assistant coach,
Shanna, who had graduated the year before.

Shanna laughed and shouted something as she pointed the hose
at one of the other girls, soaking her T-shirt.

At least her T-shirt was black. Shanna had on a white one, and
it was wet enough that a person could see right through it. Ellen
focused her gaze back on Cheerio and her apples.

"This is a different cow than the one you had at the parade," a
voice said beside her.

She forced a smile on her face and turned to look at Travis.

"Good eyes," she said simply. Somehow when she was around Travis, she felt like such a child for having such a passion for her cows. He made her want to be more worldly, more...sensuous or something.

Things that she knew she would never be. She didn't know how to flirt, and she didn't have the time or inclination to be interested in the things that most girls her age were interested in.

Normally she was happy with herself that way, but when she was around Travis, she desperately wanted to be whatever it was that he wanted her to be.

That wasn't healthy. Or, maybe it wasn't entirely true. She just desperately wanted him to like her.

Frustrated with herself, she looked away.

"Bad day?" he asked, taking one of the pieces of apple from her hand, and holding it out for Cheerio, who had just swallowed the last apple slice Ellen had given her and was looking for another piece.

"No. It's a good day. We just sold a cow, and it looks like Uncle Tadgh might be on the verge of selling a few more."

"Everyone likes your Uncle Tadgh. I've heard that since he's gotten married, he's become even more successful. And, I've heard that he credits his wife."

"I love her," Ellen said sincerely.

"But don't you feel left out?" Travis asked, which made her narrow her eyes and look at him.

That was not a typical question she would expect from a teenage boy.

"No. Ashley goes out of her way to make sure I'm included."

"I would think they'd act like newlyweds, and that would make me uncomfortable." He shivered, and she didn't think it was put on.

She had heard that his mom went from boyfriend to boyfriend, and it stood to reason that she had several of them over to her house. Maybe that's the way she acted with her boyfriend, and it made Travis feel like he wasn't as important to her.

"I guess they probably do. They hold hands, and they always love being with each other. Whatever Tadgh is doing, Ashley wants to be with him, and vice versa."

"That's annoying."

"It makes me happy. Uncle Tadgh smiles a lot more than he ever did, and Ashley makes everyone laugh. She's always in a good mood. I want to be just like her when I grow up."

That was true. She hadn't really thought about how someone could set the tone of the house with the way they act, and their attitude. But Ashley did.

She made their house a home, not just with the homely touches and the little decorations she put up, the cooking she did in the kitchen, and the way there was always a snack waiting for Ellen when she got home from school, but because of the smiles and the laughter and the way she never got upset over anything. Even when Ashley had dropped a whole bowl of Jello salad yesterday, salad that Ashley had spent several hours making, she just laughed and said that accidents happened, and then she dropped to her knees and started to clean it up.

Of course, Uncle Tadgh had come over to help, which Ellen supposed any woman would appreciate in a husband, and together they knelt on the floor. It ended up being fun family time as they laughed and Ashley told the story about one time when she had dropped the fruit salad her mother had just made for a bridal shower, and her mother had scooped it all up put it back in the bowl and taken it to the shower anyway.

It had been a horrifying story, but also funny the way Ashley told it, and Ashley had them in stitches. Of course, she promised them that she was not going to scoop all the Jello up from the floor and serve it for supper. But, after they'd eaten, they all got in the car and went to Sweet Water and dumped the Jello salad in Munchie's bowl.

Something that could have been a major problem and caused a lot of hardship and hard will, causing fighting and yelling in a normal home, had ended up being a great family evening and lots of fun.

"I think you need to be just like yourself when you grow up," Travis said, his voice sounded a little bit distracted.

Ellen had started to smile, but she looked over at him, and saw that his gaze was not directed at her, but instead he looked at the cheerleaders and the water fight they were having with the hose.

Figures. He was still stuck on Shanna.

Ellen sighed in her soul, telling herself that she wouldn't be jealous, she wouldn't be angry, and she wouldn't think mean thoughts about Shanna.

Instead, she'd try to be a friend.

"She's pretty," Ellen said, looking over at Shanna, whose cropped T-shirt was wet and sticking to her skin.

She forced herself not to look away, but to think about things that she could do that would help Travis. Something to get Shanna to notice him. That's who he really wanted. She hadn't been a very good friend, since she hadn't tried to help them get together at all.

"So are you," Travis said. Ellen didn't even look at him.

She could tell from listening to his voice that he had looked back down.

"So, you like blue eyes?"

"Sure," he said easily.

"Mine are green."

She held out her hand so Cheerio could take another bite of apple.

"I like green better than blue."

"You don't have to come over here and try to say a bunch of things that aren't true. I'll be your friend regardless of whether you think my eyes are pretty or not."

There. She said it kind of nicely. At least she didn't sound bitter or angry, the way she felt. The way she mostly felt.

That was a start. Uncle Tadgh always said that if she acted the way she was supposed to, the right feelings would come in time.

Travis moved, going to the other side of Cheerio, his back toward the cheerleaders.

"Is that better?" he asked, smiling a little, but looking a bit pained.

"You can look at them if you want to. I was just trying to think how I can get Shanna to notice you. I don't exactly run in her circles, and I probably don't have any sway with her, but if you think of something I can do to help, I'm happy to."

There. There was an offer that she really didn't want to make, but it was the kind of offer a friend would make.

"I told you at the parade, I like to look at her, but I don't really like her. I know you probably don't understand, but there's a difference."

"Oh I understand," she said.

And she did. She figured Shanna was probably what a man would consider eye candy. Something that looked good, but didn't have a whole lot of nutrition.

Maybe it was a woman thing, but she wanted to not just have nutrition, but to look good, too. She didn't want to be a boring vegetable, that someone ate just because I had to, not because they wanted to.

"You're the one who doesn't understand," she mumbled.

"Then make me," Travis said. His words weren't as easy as they usually were.

Her head jerked up and tilted slightly. How could she explain?

"That's a huge compliment to a girl when you look at her the way you do. Whether you mean it, or whether you don't, women like to have that kind of attention. Shanna doesn't really care what you say to me, because you're saying something different, something better, when you look at her like that."

That might not be the best way to explain it, but it was the only way she could come up with.

He seemed like he was digesting that, unsure how to answer her. She figured he hadn't thought of it like that before, just from the way he seemed to be chewing on the idea in his mind.

"Is there a problem with that?" he finally said.

"Not now. But when you're with someone, a girl, and you look at another girl the way you look at Shanna, it's an insult to the girl that you're with."

"An insult?"

"Sure. Like you're standing here, but you'd rather be over there."

"And that's an insult?"

"You don't want some girl to be with you, while she admires someone else, right?" Ellen didn't think that it was that hard to understand. It was just basically a do unto others as you would have them do unto you situation.

"No. But I'm not really admiring Shanna. I told you, I like the way she looks, but I don't really like her."

"But the way she looks is a part of her. It's the whole package. You can't really separate it, and... I think there's something in every woman that wants to be admired for the way she looks. Or at least, admired for the way she looks inside. But, as long as you don't have any other girl, it doesn't really matter. You can admire whoever you want to admire."

"I'm not admiring her!" Travis said, and for the first time he sounded at least a little angry.

"Maybe, maybe not, but you look like you are," Ellen said simply, feeding Cheerio the last of the apple. Then she brushed her hands down her pant legs. If the girls hadn't been playing with the hose, she would hose her hands off.

"I try not to, but she just seems to draw my eye."

"Maybe you like her better than what you think you do."

"No. I just like to look at her. But you're probably right, it would be better to just not."

"You can do whatever you want to," Ellen said.

"I want to talk to you," Travis said, bending his head down over Cheerio's back, like he was trying to catch her eye.

"You are."

"Without talking about Shanna too."

"I only talked about her because you were looking at her."

"That's why I moved over here, so I wouldn't be tempted to look at her. Because I don't want to."

"I see," Ellen said, although she really didn't. If he had to move to a different position so he wouldn't look at Shanna, it still meant that he wanted to. He was just forcing himself to not.

But maybe that was like her, going into the store and avoiding the candy aisle. If she didn't see the Twinkies, she didn't want to buy them. She supposed that was kind of the same thing.

"I was just wondering if the next time there's a parade, if your Uncle Tadgh wants there to be two cows in it, I'll lead one with you again if you want," Travis said.

His voice trailed off a little, like he thought maybe she'd laugh at him.

"I think he'd really like that," Ellen said.

"And, not asking you out on a date or anything, but I get paid on Friday, and usually I buy ice cream for my brothers, and if you happen to be in town on Friday night, I'll get some for you too."

He couldn't ask her out on a date. Her uncle would never let her date. Not at thirteen. But his statement made her smile.

"Just a friends thing. Because we're friends." He paused, his hands stopping in the middle of Cheerio's back, as he had been swiping down it. "We are friends, right?"

"Yeah. I consider you a friend."

"That's good. Because I consider you a friend too."

Chapter 24

"There's a drought in Texas, and they're culling cows down there because they don't have enough hay to feed them. You can bet the price is going to go up." Miller Carthwright spoke as he reached for the pot of mashed potatoes.

"I've heard the same thing. That's why I think it's a good idea for us to invest in some cattle. Or, not so much investing, as allowing Zeke to bring the three hundred head he got a hold of out here." Baker grabbed a saltshaker and passed it to Miller as he spoke.

Jonah had made mashed potatoes, but he forgot to put salt in them.

That was the least of his worries. He had spoken with Darby, and they agreed that it would probably be best for him to break the information that he had gotten married, and that he was also a father, to the guys alone.

So Darby had stayed in town this evening, making a video with the old coots, while Amber played with her friends at the diner.

As much as Jonah wanted his little family to be together, and as much as he was almost positive his friends would be happy for him, he agreed with Darby that would be a good idea for him to tell them while Amber wasn't there.

She'd already been through enough, and he didn't want her to be upset even more.

Of course, the fact that she'd been through so much, made him want to be with her, but Darby assured him that they would be together for the rest of their lives. One more evening apart to get things straightened out would not hurt anything and would actually be good.

"The problem is I'm not sure when Zeke's gonna come," Gideon said, holding a bite of the meat gravy Jonah had made in the air, looking at it but not really seeing it. It was obvious he was thinking about their plans for the ranch.

"Whether he comes out or not, he was sending his cattle as soon as we said it was a go," Jonah said, trying to put his head in the conversation.

He had things he wanted to talk about, but this was their livelihood, and it meant almost as much to him as the happiness of his family. He needed to be able to support them.

"I was really thinking a dude ranch might be a good idea," Baker said, sounding casual, but looking around at the table, knowing that it was an idea that no one had talked about before, and he might get some pushback on it.

Miller responded immediately. "I think that's a great idea. You're talking about having tourists come out and pay to stay and be shown around the ranch?"

"That's right. We're doing the work anyway. We might as well have people come look at us while we're doing it." Miller grinned, shoving potatoes in his mouth.

"You need somewhere to house them." Jonah said, adding to the conversation. Not against the idea, but just wanting them to consider every angle. He liked to know what he was up against before he made any moves in his business.

"The old bunkhouse. And there's the old house that Zeke and Baker and Miller and I were going to move into." Gideon spoke easily, not in a combative way, but in a constructive way that said they were discussing things.

He appreciated that about his group of friends. He had been with people who needed to have their way, or they got angry and had more of a shouting conversation, if he could call it conversation at all.

Jonah didn't mind discussing things, and he didn't mind supporting other people's ideas. He wanted to do things based on merit, not based on someone's ego because they had thrown an idea out.

"I have to put an addition on to some woman's house outside of town, then I figured I'd get started on the house that we'll be living in."

Jonah leveled his gaze at Gideon. "I didn't say you guys had to move out of here."

"You want some privacy with your new wife, don't you?" Baker asked, lifting his brows.

"Well, about that," Jonah started.

"She wants to have your marriage annulled already?" Gideon asked with a smirk. "Is that why she's not here tonight?"

"No. Actually, it's kind of the opposite."

"What's the opposite of getting a marriage annulled?" Gideon said, scratching his head.

"Not the opposite in that way, just the opposite as in there's more, rather than less." Jonah knew that didn't make sense, and he hurried on before anyone could question him about it. "I have a daughter."

"What?" Miller said, acting like he really hadn't heard.

"When my ex left me, she was pregnant. She didn't mention it to me, and I had no idea. Darby, the woman I married, happened to adopt my daughter, and that was what she was doing out here - looking for me."

"You...didn't marry her because you loved her?" Baker asked, almost as though he couldn't believe it. Surely he knew that there were people who got married for reasons other than love all the time. Weren't there?

He thought so, but he honestly wasn't sure.

"I think love will come in time, but she came looking for me, and we decided that the best thing that we could do for our daughter - since Darby legally adopted her - was for us to get married."

"That's like a marriage of convenience. I've heard of those." Miller nodded his head thoughtfully.

"I guess it is. But I have every intention of treating her like our marriage is just as real as anyone else's."

He didn't know what else to say. That he had every intention of treating her like he loved her because he had every intention of loving her? They might not understand that. Understand the idea that love was an action, and not just a feeling.

"I think that's a smart thing to do. As long as you two are compatible, at least believe the same, have the same morals and values, you'll probably have a better marriage with her than you had with your ex anyway. At least you have as much of a chance of not getting divorced." Baker's words sounded wise and thoughtful.

"That's what we're hoping. I...wanted to introduce her to you guys, since you all just got in, but we thought it might be best for me to let you know what we did, because we didn't want Amber to see a bunch of bad reactions."

"Sounds like the little girl's been through enough," Gideon said easily.

Of all of his friends, Gideon was the one who acted most like a child, but he was also the one who seemed to get along best with children.

That just made sense since Gideon was always ready with a laugh and a smile and unlike some people who were always joking, he didn't seem to have a temper. At least not one that Jonah had ever seen.

"All right, so you're married, and you have a daughter. You don't mess around," Baker said with a slight smile. "Does this change anything?" he asked, his words sounding serious.

"I'm not expecting it to. Of course I want to be home more, but work is work, and it needs to get done."

"Having the cattle will keep us home," Baker pointed out.

"That's true. Three hundred head sounds like a lot." Jonah wasn't sure he wanted to get into the cattle that deep, but if there was a drought in the South, it almost certainly would make prices go up. It might be a good time to jump in. "Do any of us know anything about raising cattle?"

"Zeke does. And I grew up out east on a farm. It's a little bit different. I think the water issues are the main thing. Back in Virginia, even in a drought, we still had water for our cows. It's everywhere."

"Yeah. Water rights are little bit touchier around here." Miller's lips flattened, but he didn't look hopeless. "I think we can make it work though. We have enough ground, between the four of us, with the other guys pitching in, that we ought to be fine. If we're not, surely we can hold off selling anything until prices start to go up."

"Regardless, we can get some horses, fix up the old bunkhouse and the house we'll be living in, and we'll make a nice side profit. With the dude ranch, along with the crop dusting and the cattle, there should be something for everyone." Baker looked around the table.

Jonah appreciated the fact that all the men wanted to make sure that they would all be able to raise families on the ranch. That it wasn't just about supporting a bunch of bachelors, but it was about generating enough income through diversification so that they could each get married and have children and the ranch would support them.

"You know for the last few conventions we were at over the winter, our focus was booking people specifically around our area, trying to stay home as much as we could. I think we were successful, and if we focus on growing that part of our business, there might come a point where no one will have to stay out more than a night or two," Gideon said. His eyes focused on Jonah. After all, Jonah was the one right now who was married and would be most reluctant to leave his wife and daughter.

"I like the idea of having cattle and even some other animals on the ranch and building up that part of it."

"Horses. Tourists love horses," Miller said confidently.

"They probably do, but I don't know anything about them," Jonah admitted.

"I do. It's been a few years, but at one point, before I joined the Air Force, I had considered being a professional bronc rider."

"I always knew you were a little nuts," Gideon said to Miller.

Miller grinned. "Can't deny it. But, I think I've got a little bit more mature over the years, and if I'm going to take a risk, I want a bigger chance of it paying off."

"And you think getting cattle will pay off?" Jonah said, really having no idea. He knew they could make a go with the crop dusting, although if they tried to stay within half a day's drive, it might be harder. Still, he thought they could make it work. But the cattle, he had no idea.

"I think the only thing we can do is try. We'll just do what we did with the crop dusting, because before we started that, we really didn't know anything about it other than how to fly and work on airplanes. So, it can't be that much harder." Gideon gave a confident grin.

They continued to talk for a little bit, and Jonah followed the conversation, figuring that it would have been fine for Amber and Darby to be here. The guys had accepted the fact that he was married and that he had a daughter without much fanfare at all.

It was a struggle to pay attention because he wanted to know what Darby thought about what they were talking about. About the idea of a dude ranch. About having horses and tourists and possibly opening up the ranch to something that, while it would keep them home or, would invite strangers into their home and privacy.

He thought she would be okay with it, and then he thought of something else.

"Darby used to be a caterer. If we end up going with the dude ranch idea, I'd have to check with her, but I bet she'd be interested in at least being in charge of the menu, if not the cooking itself. I know she loved it but had to sell it when she left Maryland."

"That would be pretty awesome and one thing we don't have to think about," Miller said easily.

"I'll have to check with her. Also, I know you guys just got in today, but I promised Darby and Amber that we'd leave tomorrow afternoon to drive to The Cities to get a piano."

"A piano?" Baker rubbed his chin.

"Yeah. Amber plays."

He didn't say anything more. He supposed if they hung around enough, they'd hear her. But, bragging about his daughter's gift wasn't something he was going to engage in. At least not now.

He was proud of her, and wanted the world to know, but he also didn't want her to be overwhelmed by a lot of attention. But his friends would support and love her, and that would go a long way toward developing a great relationship all around.

"Well, I figured we'd all be moved out of here tomorrow, so 'till you get back, the place will be yours."

"I haven't been over to the other house for a while, but if it turns out that it's uninhabitable, you know you're welcome to stay. I don't want for me to get married and then everybody has to leave."

No one seemed upset.

"We'll be out for a while anyway. We'll figure things out after you guys have a few months to yourselves. Might be that everybody works better in a house of their own, and we have enough ground. We can talk about it." Baker's words were easy, and Jonah figured they truly didn't care. They'd lived in some pretty tight and cramped places, and as long as the roof didn't leak and the water was good to drink and it didn't get too cold in the winter, he couldn't imagine any of them complaining.

Jonah couldn't wait to get away from the table, wanting to go to his wife, and he left shortly after, since he had told Darby that he'd drive into town to pick her up.

Amber was going to go to school tomorrow, then they would pick her up and they'd go straight to The Cities from there. He had a lot to talk about with Darby, and he couldn't wait to start.

Chapter 25

"So is that the piano you want?" the salesman asked, glancing at his watch. Darby figured he was trying to do it inconspicuously.

It was ten minutes until time for the store to close, and Amber was still playing the piano.

"Yes. That's the one." Darby smiled, although she was tired.

It had been a long day, with getting Amber ready for school, meeting Jonah's friends, talking about the ranch... She had to admit she was excited about the idea of having a dude ranch, having people in and cooking and creating menus and meals and cowboy food.

It wasn't something she did much back east, and while she loved her catering business, she loved the idea that she would be branching out and doing different things. Loved the idea of experimenting in the kitchen, finding recipes and tweaking them to suit their brand.

She could admit she had been extremely excited.

Jonah had smiled indulgently at her, and she reminded herself that she wanted to thank him for mentioning her background in catering and cooking.

She hadn't had a chance, since they had barely had lunch before it was time to go pick Amber up at school - they'd gotten permission to take her out a couple of hours early - then they'd gone to The Cities, eaten a bit, and spent hours here at the music store.

Amber could spend hours more.

"I'm sorry. It's just been so long since she's been able to play the piano. I know she's really enjoying it."

The salesman nodded, and while the entire store had been awed at Amber's ability, the salesman had a family he wanted to go home to.

"If you get the paperwork together, we'll sign for the delivery and pay the bill," Jonah said, and she was grateful that he was moving things along.

The salesman nodded, mumbled a few words about getting a delivery date together and hurried off.

"She's had a lot of chaos in her life, maybe that's part of the reason she's playing so much," Jonah said low, after the salesman left.

It warmed her heart that he had listened and realized that Amber processed her feelings through the music that she played.

"I'm sure you're right. I haven't seen or heard anything from Nora..." she allowed her words to trail off, inviting him to tell her whether he had.

He took the hint, and said, "Me neither."

He didn't look overly concerned about it, and they'd had such a good time, laughing and joking and enjoying themselves, not just on the ride to The Cities, but at the music store too, as they looked at different pianos. Amber had a lot of fun explaining the different styles and sounds of the pianos to Jonah, to whom all of that was new. He had seemed extremely interested and had paid attention to everything Amber had said.

If he always paid attention the same way he'd been paying attention in the past few days, which Darby had no doubt he would, he would soon know as much about music and pianos as she did. That seemed to be his goal. He wanted to know his daughter. And he didn't just say it, but he lived it.

She loved that about him.

Amber's music switched from an up-tempo Bach fugue to a slower, more romantic piece.

"Want to dance?" Jonah asked, surprising her.

She looked around the store. It was mostly empty, although there were a couple of last-minute sales going on at the front counter.

She almost shook her head no. She didn't want to dance in front of an audience, but she'd been having such a good time, not only did she not want to tell him no, but she wanted to be closer. That seemed like a good excuse.

He held his hand out, and she slipped hers into his.

She hadn't expected the rush of tingles that went up her arm as his fingers closed around hers and their hands slid together.

She held his eyes, although her gaze was tempted to lower and look at her hand, see if it was glowing or something. That's what it felt like.

He pulled her in until she was almost against him, then slid his arm around her waist. She put her hand on his shoulder, and they started swaying gently to the music.

"I like this song. I think I'll ask Amber to play it every night."

She smiled as his lips quirked. He wasn't joking, she didn't think, just saying something to lighten the mood a little. They couldn't be too serious in the middle of the music store. Although she wanted to be.

"I assumed we would get one hotel room with two beds. That's if you're okay sharing a bed with Amber?" he asked, and she appreciated that he wasn't pushing her for a more intimate sleeping relationship arrangement, and she also didn't want two hotel rooms.

"Yes. That sounds perfect."

"All right. That's kind of what I was thinking, but I thought it would be best if we talked about it. I... I have a tendency to want to make decisions on my own, so if I forget to ask. It's not because I don't want your input. It's just because I'm not used to having to remember."

"Same. But you've been very considerate. More considerate than I have been, I think. Regardless of that, I had a great time."

"I really enjoy spending time with you and Amber. You have a great relationship with her, the kind of relationship I wish I had with my mom."

"Maybe that's because she's adopted, and because I knew from the beginning that if I hadn't stepped in, she wouldn't be with us. I don't know."

"That might have something to do with it, but I think you just naturally have a confidence about you and she respects you, but she also likes you. It's obvious. And it's fun to watch."

"She's going to like you, too. In fact, she already does. After all, you kept your word about the pianos and taking us to get one. You have no idea how much that means to her."

"I might have a little idea. I can hear her heart while she's playing right now, and... I don't know if this is supposed to be a romantic song, but it really feels like it."

"It does to me as well," she said, lifting her head. Her temple brushed his cheek, and his breath blew by her ear.

He smelled good, like the outdoors and strength and character, and his shoulder was hard under her hand, his hand firm on her back. He felt like the kind of man she could trust. The kind of man she was privileged to be able to marry.

He wouldn't have married you if you hadn't adopted his daughter.

She tried to shove that little thought aside. It might be true. They certainly wouldn't be married if she hadn't adopted Amber. But she wouldn't have come out West to find him if it weren't for Amber. So what did it matter whether he married her because she was Amber's mom, or because he loved her?

Because you want someone to love you. Not just want you for the kid that you have.

"What made you tense just now?" Jonah asked, his voice right by her ear, his hand holding firm on her back, his other hand holding hers.

"How could you tell?" she asked, as much to give her time to think of an answer as because she was curious as to how he knew.

"I felt you. You're close enough. Surely it's not a surprise that you tense and I can tell with as close as we are."

"I guess not."

She didn't say anything, hoping he'd forget his question, deliberately trying to make herself relax so she wouldn't remind him that he hadn't gotten an answer to the first one.

She should have known that he really was interested in her and her reactions and her thoughts and feelings.

She wasn't sure whether anyone had ever shown that kind of interest in her before. She had to admit, she liked it. And she also had to admit that it didn't seem like he was interested just because of Amber. After all, he hadn't had to dance with her. He didn't have to hold her close and care about whether or not she was tensing.

"Are you going to answer me?" he prompted her.

"I don't know what to say. I ... I'm afraid it will come out as a criticism, and I don't mean it that way."

"Try me," he said easily.

"I love this. I love that you're holding me. I love that we're dancing together. I feel like you're the kind of man that I can trust and depend on, and I love it."

"I don't understand why that would have upset you," he said.

"Because I had a little thought go through my head that you're just holding me, you just married me, you're just here today because of Amber."

This time she felt him tense, and his head lifted just a bit. Not enough that she could see his eyes, but enough that she could feel him pull away from her just a bit.

"That was what I was afraid of. I didn't mean it to push you away, I'm just being honest. I didn't mean to think that thought, and I was fighting it. Because, after all, I wouldn't be out here if it weren't for Amber. I wouldn't have looked you up if it weren't for her, and I wouldn't have married you so fast if it weren't for her. I...I would have married you eventually, if you had wanted to."

Those last words were said softly, hesitantly, like she wasn't sure whether she wanted to admit them or not. It felt like being vulnerable, and while she trusted him, she wasn't sure she could trust him with that much vulnerability.

"Everything you said was true. I can't deny any of it."

She didn't mean to sigh, but it came from the bottom of her lungs, pushed out sadly.

"But I love the way you feel in my arms. I love the way you've raised my little girl. Our little girl." He corrected himself, emphasizing the "our."

"I love your smile. I love how excited you were today about a dude ranch. How you jumped in and were on board with all of the ideas. I didn't have to talk you into them, or beg you to stay, or ask you to reconsider. You just..."

"I *was* excited. It wasn't pretending."

"I know. I didn't mean that."

"I want to be involved in what you do. If we're going to be married, if you're going to be a father to my daughter, if we're going to make this work –"

"We are. We are and we are. It is going to work. We're going to make sure of it."

"Then I'm excited to be able to work with you. I'm excited that we're going to do it together. I'm excited that you're including me with what your friends are doing. I didn't feel like I was the fifth wheel. I felt like I was part of the group. And that was because you deliberately made sure that I did. And I really appreciated that."

"I guess that's what I'm saying. Maybe it's because of Amber that we met. And maybe it's because of Amber that we're married right now, but it's because of you and who you are and what you are, what you do, the character you have, and the beauty and grace in your heart, that draws me to you. That makes me want to dance with you. Actually, I'd like to do more than dance with you right now, but I don't suppose the music store is the best place for our first kiss."

"I don't suppose," she said, rather breathless, and she actually wouldn't have cared if he kissed her in the music store. Or wherever. Just as long as he did it.

Why don't you tell him?

Now that was an idea she could get behind.

If she could trust him with everything else that she told him, she could certainly trust him to tell him that she wanted to kiss him, right?

"I have the papers you need to sign. I have a delivery date, as well, if we can check it out and see what works for you." The salesman interrupted them, and Darby had to bite her lip to keep from voicing her disappointment.

But, as Jonah's arms fell away from her, slowly, far more slowly than normal, his hand twisted in hers, so that he was holding it.

He looked down, as she looked up, and he smiled at her.

Her heart thumped, and maybe her smile trembled just a little, but it wasn't because she wasn't sure whether or not she wanted to hold his hand. It was because she couldn't believe how good it felt. How much it scrambled her insides. How natural it seemed at the same time.

They walked over, as Amber continued to play, while the salesman went over the delivery options, and Darby got her checkbook out of her purse.

She wrote the check out while Jonah confirmed the delivery date - Wednesday of that week. He chose the soonest one, and she could only assume that he was going to make his schedule fit theirs, because he knew how important having a piano was to Amber.

Just one more thing she needed to remember to thank him for. She appreciated his consideration and his thoughtfulness as well. Even when he didn't necessarily understand, and even when it was inconvenient, he made sure he put Amber first.

He had done the same with her also. It seemed that he wanted to make sure they were taken care of, and he would put his needs aside if that was what it took.

Having that kind of care shown for her made her want to care about him in the same way. To put his needs first, to take care of him, and make sure she was doing everything she could to make his life easier and happier.

She could only imagine that would create a positive spiral for the length of their relationship, as long as they continued in that way.

She determined to try. To try not to let criticisms, or unkind words, or complaints sour their relationship.

Of course there would be times where they would have to talk about things that weren't pleasant, but there really shouldn't be any time where she *had* to complain or criticize.

If she could accept him the way he was and pray about the things she felt needed to be changed, then pray and ask God if it wasn't Jonah that needed to be changed, but her. If she could do that, she could imagine that their relationship would get better and sweeter with each passing year.

That was her goal anyway. A worthy goal, she thought.

Chapter 26

It was well past closing time by the time they had made the arrangements for delivery, paid for the piano, gotten the receipt, and coaxed Amber away from it.

Her eyes were glowing, and she practically levitated out of the door. But, unsurprising to Darby, by the time they'd had a small bite to eat, and Amber had taken a shower, she was drooping.

Jonah had walked them to the room, then told them that he would find something to do for an hour or so while they got ready for bed.

By the time she was finished with her shower, and snuggled in bed beside her daughter, Amber was snoring.

The door clicked, and out of habit, Darby tensed.

It was almost certainly Jonah, but she didn't relax until his tall figure shown in the doorway.

"Everything good?"

"Yeah. She's asleep already. Big day."

"I can hear her snoring. That's cute."

"Yeah. When she lies on her back, she always snores."

"She went to sleep that fast?" Jonah said, padding across the room to his duffle that he had set against the wall.

"Playing the piano relaxes her. She always goes to sleep easily after she's had an hour or two to play."

"She played at least that much today, probably more."

"Thank you for your patience. I don't think there are a lot of men in the world who would have spent five hours allowing their daughter to play dozens of different pianos to figure out which one she wanted."

"I think she knew which one she wanted the moment she touched it. She just played the other ones because she enjoyed it. And I enjoyed listening to her."

"Thank you for saying so."

"And, just so we're clear, it's not every man that has a daughter with that kind of talent. What's the saying? With great privilege comes great responsibility?"

"Something like that."

"God entrusted me with the two most wonderful women in the world. You're here in this hotel room with me right now. I need to rise to the challenge a little, don't you think?"

She could hear the smile in his voice, even though it was too dark to see him. She had left the bathroom light on for him, but it was the only light in the room.

"I think you're pretty special."

Darby rolled her eyes when she said that. He'd just called her the most wonderful woman in the world, and she came back with 'I think you're pretty special?'

"Thanks."

"Jonah?"

"Yeah?"

"You're more than pretty special. You are...the best. Literally."

That was a little bit better. Still, it wasn't the compliment she wanted to give. She wanted to tell him...that she loved him? She wanted to say it. But they hadn't known each other that long. Could she say it that soon?

She pressed her lips closed.

"Thanks. I'm ...going to shower and then I'll be out."

"All right."

She listened to him moving around in the bathroom, smiling a little at how perfect it felt, and yet different as well. She wasn't used to sharing a room with a man. She had to admit she liked it. Even though it would take a little getting used to.

Maybe it would always be special. Knowing there was someone else beside her. Someone else helping her raise her child. It was a beautiful thing to stand beside someone, having that person be shoulder to shoulder with her and doing life together.

She hadn't realized how much she'd longed for that, and how good it would feel to have someone who cared about her as much, or possibly more, than he cared about himself.

Even better, even more amazing, was that she had found the one man in the world who would love her daughter just as much as she did. Who would fight to get the best for her, no matter what.

Darby wasn't so naïve as to think that they would agree all the time about what the best for Amber really was, but she didn't think it mattered. As long as she knew that Jonah was working to have the best for Amber, it didn't have to match what she thought the best was.

She said a small prayer, thanking the Lord for how He'd worked things out in her life. Worked them out in a way that she would never have thought in a million years could actually happen. Even when she was looking for Jonah, she never dreamed she'd be married to him.

Never dreamed that he would treat her the way he was. That he would be so considerate and thoughtful to Amber as well.

There was something she needed to say to him. Something she didn't want to wait any longer to say. So, when he came out of the shower, she was going to talk to him.

"Do you need this light on?" he asked just a few minutes later as he stepped out of the bathroom.

"No."

The light went down without him saying anything more. Before her eyes had adjusted to the darkness, he'd slipped under the covers in the bed beside her.

"Thank you for a really great day," he said, not sounding the slightest bit tired.

"Thank you," she murmured, not able to think of anything to add to it. Maybe that was just because she was nervous about what she was about to say.

"Jonah?"

"Hmm?" he murmured.

"I know that I had said that I would share a room with Amber back at the ranch. But... I was thinking that maybe it would be a good idea for you and me to share a room to begin with. So there would be no awkward switching at any point. I am not saying that I want..."

Her voice trailed off while she tried to think of a delicate way to put it.

"I think I get it. You just want to share a room, not necessarily move our relationship into the physical, just keep that part of our relationship private."

"Exactly. If I'm in your room, no one will know what's going on. But if I'm in Amber's room, until I decide to move into yours, it's going to be like waving flags around."

"I think the guys are moving to the smaller house we have. So they'll probably not be there, but I still think that's a good idea. What's between you and me will stay between you and me."

"That, and... I guess I just feel like I can trust you. I know it's only been a short time, but everything you've done has been with you thinking about Amber and me before you think of yourself. I feel like this will be something else that I can trust you in."

There was no fear in her at all. A little bit of nervousness, sure, but she wasn't worried. She knew she was making the right decision. She hadn't had such assurance about a decision for a really long time. But there was no question in her mind that this was the right thing to do, and that they would be safe and she could depend on him to not take advantage of her in any way.

"I don't know that I deserve that kind of trust, but I appreciate it."

"You've earned it."

"You just said we haven't been together that long. I...I want to think that this is the kind of man I always am, but I'm not perfect."

"And I don't expect you to be. I sure hope you're not thinking I'm perfect."

"Actually, I thought you were," he said, with a smile in his voice.

"I guess that's a compliment?"

"Yeah. It is. I look at you, and I see everything I'd always wanted in a woman. Everything. It's kind of crazy that God had you adopt Amber, and then look me up. I... I just can't believe how He orchestrated these things in my life. You...make me want to be better. And that's something else I can't believe. I love the guys, love my crew, but they've never made me want to be a better person. Maybe a better crewmember, better in my job, but never better from the inside out. That's what I want when I'm with you."

"That's funny, since I was just thinking basically the same thing. Only I was thinking about our relationship. How you set the standard. You have treated me far better than I deserve to be treated. With kindness and consideration, and you love my daughter. Our daughter. You love her, and you put her above yourself. You make me want to be a better parent, and a better woman. A better partner. A better spouse."

She could hear him smile, hear him huff out a small breath, and she didn't think he was laughing at her as much is it made him happy. Happy that they found each other, that they seemed to bring out the best in each other. That maybe their marriage wouldn't be a struggle with one of them constantly giving up for the other, who constantly took.

There were marriages like that. Marriages where one person grew and became a better person because they didn't have a choice, but had to if they wanted to stay married.

That kind of marriage would certainly grow a person, but it didn't fulfill a human's desire for love and romance that God had put inside, of women, especially.

Whatever a man's needs were, maybe just to be loved and respected, or maybe to be cherished as well, she wasn't sure, but she hoped Jonah found whatever he needed in her.

"The piano is coming Wednesday, so I thought that we'd go to the feed store Monday after school and get some chicks. What do you think?"

"I think that's a great idea. I think Amber is going to be really excited about it." She chuckled. "All right. I admit, *I'm* really excited about it."

"Maybe you won't believe it, but I'm excited about it too. I can't say that I've always wanted chicks. That wouldn't be the slightest bit true, but I can say now that we've talked about it, I think it's going to be a lot of fun."

"I think it will be a draw when we get the dude ranch going. People will love the fact that we have our own eggs. Plus, chickens are just fun to watch."

"I can totally see us sitting on the porch in the evening, watching the chickens in the yard while Amber plays. Maybe there will be more children eventually."

"Maybe," she said, hoping that there would be.

"I guess we didn't really talk about that. You want more kids?" he asked, and his voice sounded a little uncertain. "Amber's old enough that maybe you're looking forward to her growing up and leaving and you being done with your job."

"No. I'd like more kids. Amber always wanted brothers or sisters, and, while any children we had would be too young to really be great playmates, at least we'd have a family. I... I had considered adopting more children," she admitted, and that was not something that she had ever talked to anyone about before.

He didn't seem taken back by the idea at all, since he responded immediately. "I love that idea. If it hadn't been for you adopting, I would have lost my daughter and not even known it. I guess the idea of adopting, even older children, makes me happy."

"Then yeah. Maybe we can adopt two, and plan to have two of our own?" She was just throwing something out there, since she really had no plan.

"That sounds good to me. I...I'm not sure how to get started, but I'm sure we can figure something out."

"I'm sure we can," she said, and they lapsed into silence.

She'd managed to talk to him about everything she wanted, and it seemed like those might have been things that he wanted too, or at least would consider.

She said a prayer of thanks, feeling more blessed than she'd ever felt in her life before. Even the thought of Nora, and the complications that she might bring, couldn't dim her happiness. Nora just needed to know the Lord. Maybe, maybe they could help her get to know him.

The idea made her happy and she fell asleep with a smile on her face.

Chapter 27

Nora walked down the street sidewalk in Sweet Water, North Dakota. Three little girls came toward her, and she pretended to gaze in the window of what looked like a barbershop, hoping they would go on by without saying anything to her.

In the short amount of time that she spent in Sweet Water, she'd figured out it was one of those small towns where everyone knew everyone else and everyone talked to everyone else.

She didn't hate it exactly. It just made her uncomfortable.

She really didn't want everyone to know her. There wasn't a lot of good to know. She didn't want people to know how nasty and mean she felt inside sometimes.

"We're not going to stop looking until we find someone," one of the girls said.

Nora had been at the diner, and she recognized two of the girls, thinking maybe the older one was Sorrell and the younger one was Merritt, daughters of the diner owners.

She wasn't sure what the name of the taller of the three girls was, and she was pretty sure she hadn't seen her at the diner.

The taller girl said, "I appreciate it. I talked to my mom, and she's open to the idea. She seemed to be surprised when I told her that I wanted a dad more than anything else in the world."

"I don't know why she'd be surprised. Everyone wants a dad. No one wants to grow up without one."

"Of course not. Who else is going to teach you how to catch a ball, and tease you, and carry you around on his shoulders?"

Their words make Nora smile, bringing back sweet, buried memories of her family before her parents' divorce.

She'd wanted a dad too, when her parents split and she'd gone with her mom.

Her mom had brought in a succession of boyfriends over the years. Some of them stuck around for a while, but none stuck around forever. Maybe that was what had made her so distrustful of men.

"I wanted a dad more than anything," the tall girl said fervently, as they seemed to stop right beside Nora.

She could see them out of the corner of her eye, but she kept her gaze focused on the window, not wanting to have to talk to them.

"I know how you feel. That's exactly how we felt too. And, God answered our prayer. We'll keep praying."

Nora snorted. God had never answered any of her prayers. Of course, she couldn't really remember praying for a father as much as railing at God for not giving her one, or for taking the one that she had away.

Why hadn't her parents been able to work things out? Didn't they know how important it was for a kid to have a mom and a dad? She had a lot of anger and resentment because her parents hadn't stuck it out. What had been so terrible that two people who had once professed love for each other — she had seen the wedding photos, where they stared lovingly into each other's eyes — but then couldn't stand each other to the point where they felt they had to split, ripping their family apart, in order to get away from each other?

She resented their selfishness.

She also resented God for allowing it to happen. For allowing a little girl to lose her nice, safe, secure family, and be jerked from rental to low income rental, while her mother's boyfriends paraded in and out the door.

Unlike some children, the boyfriends had never shown an interest in her. One blessing in that miserable existence.

Although she had gone through a stage in her teenage years where she'd tried to attract their interest.

Of course, then there was her own disastrous marriage. She could blame everything on Jonah, but it wouldn't be right or fair.

Maybe the idea that she had been going to have her own child, and knew that her marriage was crumbling, and she couldn't stand the idea of her kid losing her family and father, maybe that's what had made her run.

Their marriage would have broken up regardless, but guilt that she hadn't told Jonah about his daughter plagued her. Fresh guilt after listening to the little girls talk.

Was that how Amber felt? Was that what had driven Darby to find Jonah? What had prompted them to get married?

She almost snorted. Their marriage wasn't any more likely to last than anyone else's.

"My mom said that God brought Elias and her together at the perfect time. I think He'll do the same for you."

"But mom also says that we have to pray."

"That's what my mom said. And I know that God answers prayers, just sometimes... His answer is no. That's what I'm afraid of. That I'll never get a dad."

The girls walked on, their footsteps slowly fading along with their voices.

Nora continued to stare at the shop window, not seeing anything.

"Hello. I don't think I've seen you in town before," a voice said, startling her out of her contemplations.

She turned reluctantly. She didn't feel like talking to people. She felt like examining her life and trying to figure out what she was doing wrong. Was there something different she could do? Something that would fill the gnawing ache in her chest? Something that would make her happy?

"I'm not from around here," she said, not meeting the lady's eyes, and moving like she wanted to walk past.

"Oh, I knew that. I know everyone in town. I've been here all my life." The lady held out her hand. "I'm Miss April. I couldn't help but notice that you looked a little sad. I figured I'd stop and introduce myself and invite you to come on down to the community center where my friends and I often hang out and craft together."

Nora looked at the old, wrinkled hand, before her own, much younger and smoother hand reached up to take it. She shook it slowly. "Nice to meet you Miss April. I'm Nora."

"Maybe some friendship and fellowship will cheer you up," Miss April said, and Nora couldn't help but think that she was butting into business that wasn't hers.

But you were just wondering whether there was something you could do differently? Why don't you talk to this stranger about it? It's not like she's going to judge you, since she doesn't know you and won't ever see you again.

Miss April didn't seem inclined to go anywhere, as Nora stood on the sidewalk and chewed her lip.

"I think I've made a mess of my life," she said softly.

"Oh honey, we all do that at times. Usually, there's nothing you can do that you can't undo, addictions aside. You didn't kill anyone did you?"

The question was innocent, said almost in fun, but it brought tears to Nora's eyes.

"I almost did."

The lady didn't even blink. "Well, 'almost' is a no, and we'll take that," Miss April said, nodding her head decisively.

"Yeah, that's true." Nora thought about how close she had come to killing her own child. Maybe that was why she felt so driven to butt into Amber's life and try to do the best for her. Try to help her make money while she was young enough to be sought after.

"You make mistakes, then you grow from them and you move on. Always remembering that people are more important than things, and you'll never regret putting other people ahead of yourself," Miss April said, and it sounded a lot like unsolicited advice, but Nora was at the point in her life where maybe she needed a little bit of unsolicited advice.

"It's important to make money," she said, not that she disagreed with what Miss April had said, just that Miss April was missing out on things that matter.

"Money up to a certain point is important. Enough to keep a roof over your head and food in your belly and the bills paid. Beyond that, it can cause more problems than it solves."

"Spoken by someone who has plenty of money," Nora said, and she felt bitter, knowing that came out in her words.

"I have enough to do exactly what I just said. In fact, I've always wanted to go to Italy, and recently I did take a trip. We went a half an hour away from here, where we stayed for three weeks in a relative's cabin while my husband watched TV and I sat on the porch looking at the wildlife and soaking up the sun."

"Aren't you angry that you didn't get to go to Italy? Don't you wish you had more money so that you could be happy?"

"You know, there's a part of me that still wouldn't mind going to Italy. But there's a bigger part of me that knows that the choice to be happy is mine, and it has nothing to do with how much money I have."

Miss April didn't say anything else, and she really didn't have to. Nora felt like she just had a revelation.

All of her life she'd blamed her circumstances for her unhappiness. Her parents' divorce, the dumps they lived in, the boyfriends who never stuck around.

Her husband who could never keep her happy. Who didn't even seem to try most of the time.

But, if this woman was standing here in front of her talking about her pseudo-Italian vacation, and she was saying it with a smile, saying that she still would like to go on it, but she was happy without it...maybe she was going about things all wrong.

She wanted Amber to have money so that she didn't have the problems that Nora had. But, thinking about what Miss April said, and what she overheard a little girl saying...maybe Darby was on the right track, and Amber would be happier with a dad, even if they lived in the middle of nowhere, and even if no one ever heard her play.

"So you're thinking about settling down around here?" Miss April said, like people often rolled into town and decided to make the place their home.

"No. I'm from Baltimore and have no plans on leaving the East Coast."

"You might find you like it here. If you don't have anything else to do, remember you're welcome at the community center."

"I'll remember that," Nora said. Miss April gave her hand a squeeze and gave Nora one more smile before she walked slowly away.

Nora watched her go, feeling like there were times in a person's life where something happened that changed her life forever and that this could be one of those times.

Chapter 28

"**A**mber said to tell you that her vote goes to the brisket," Jonah said as he walked into the kitchen where Darby sat at the table, her iPad in front of her, a notebook open, and her pencil poised above it.

He'd just gotten done putting Amber to bed, reading her a chapter out of the book that they'd been enjoying every evening together when he was home.

That was one job that he had completely taken over every night he was there.

His job took him away more than he liked it to, but they consoled themselves that next year would be different. Baker and Miller were going ahead and bringing the cattle, and Zeke would be arriving as well. The dude ranch was gearing up, and Darby was currently working on recipes for them.

"I think I agree with her. The brisket was definitely the best." Darby closed her notebook and looked up at him.

She had made a couple of different things for supper the last few nights, and he certainly didn't mind being the guinea pig, trying out the recipes she was interested in using for the dude ranch.

It was not a hardship at all.

Nor was it a hardship to take her in his arms and dance in the living room while their daughter played her new piano.

The piano had been delivered over a month ago, and Amber had started lessons not long after that.

The church in Sweet Water had asked her to be the Sunday evening pianist, with a regular pianist, Louise Hanson's, blessing.

It felt like things were falling into place.

Darby turned off her ipad, pushed away from the table and stood, walking easily into his arms.

Evenings were his favorite time of day, of course, where he danced with his wife and held her.

They'd done what she said, and shared a room together, but he'd given her plenty of time to get to know him, and to get used to him.

He wasn't sure how much longer it was going to take, but even though he was impatient, he had wanted to give her all the time she needed, not wanting to push her into anything that she'd regret in years to come.

"Did you have a good trip?" she asked, referring to the fact that he had been gone for two nights, and had just arrived home this evening.

"I did, I guess. Hopefully there won't be too many more times I'll have to be gone even one night, let alone, two. It was a long three days."

"It was a long two nights," she said, looking up into his eyes.

His breath hitched. And his heart started to thump.

"For me too," he said, searching her face, trying to figure out what she was saying. She looked at him like there was something she wanted him to know.

"I'm not tired," she said softly.

"Me, either." And that was completely true. He wasn't the slightest bit tired. He was thrilled to be home, and being here, right where he belonged, gave him an energy he couldn't deny.

He had opened his mouth to ask her if she'd like to take a walk, since neither one of them were tired, even though it was time to go to bed, when she said, "But I'd like to go to bed anyway."

He nodded, but there was something in her gaze that made him freeze.

"You're not tired but you want to go to bed anyway?" he said slowly, trying to figure out if there was something else she could mean by that. Something else than what he was thinking right now.

"Yes."

The word was simple, but it was the smile, a little shy, a little eager, that made his heart trip over itself and start thundering away.

"You know I am not very good at figuring these things out," he began.

"I know. And you know I'm not very good at coming right out and saying things that might get me rejected."

"I'm not going to reject you. There is no way."

She bit her lip and took a deep breath. "I want to go to bed, but I want to spend a lot of time kissing, and maybe we could find some other things to do too."

She let out her breath, like she'd just done something really hard, and her expression said she was a little afraid, waiting to see what he would say to that.

"I think that's the best idea I've heard in a really long time. I'm all for it."

And he was all for starting the kissing right now. He didn't say that though. He showed her instead, lowering his head, and kissing her the way he wanted to when he got home, but Amber was there, and he'd stopped well short of the soul-searching hello kiss he wanted to give. Bussing her cheek and brushing his lips against hers instead.

The soul deep kiss came now though, and she wrapped her arms around his neck, clinging to him, pressing herself against him, while he ran his hands down her back, and tried not to act as eager as he wanted to, but to slow down and enjoy every second of being with his wife. Enjoy the slow kiss, her little gasps of breath, her heartbeat against his, the curve of her hip and the brush of her hair as well as the feel of her body pressed to his.

All things to enjoy, to savor and cherish, all opportunities to show her, not just tell her, how much he loved her. How much there was no way he would reject her, but would welcome her and appreciate whatever she chose to give him.

She pulled back, her lips just far enough away from his that she was able to speak. "Upstairs?" she asked.

He had to laugh a little, he was just telling himself that he would stand here forever and kiss her if that's what she wanted.

"You read my mind," he said instead.

Taking her hand, they walked up the stairs together.

Enjoy this preview of *Just a Cowboy's Shotgun Wedding,* just for you!

Just a Cowboy's Shotgun Wedding

Chapter 1

"**M**ommy, Henry hit me."

"I did not! I was just swinging my arm and she got in the way."

"I'm hungry."

"Luna knocked down my block tower. Make her put it back up!"

Piper held a hand to her throbbing head and listened to the chaos of her children around her.

This was what happened when she didn't go to church. It served her right. When she rolled over in the morning and couldn't find the energy to get herself, let alone her six kids, up and ready, it always came back to bite her.

Plus, she missed the fellowship.

As a single mom who worked as hard as she could as a hairdresser, it was nice to get out and hear the Word.

She hadn't even gotten her coffee yet but had been going from crisis to crisis since she'd gotten out of bed.

Spilled milk, spilled cereal, a leaking diaper, a broken lamp, three wrestling matches, two head bumps, three Band-Aids, and that was just hitting the highlights.

The cries of her children didn't diminish as she stood at the stove, pouring pasta into the boiling water and trying to plan a grocery list in her head for the week.

Sunday afternoons were a terrible time to go grocery shopping, but she was booked solid with hairdressing clients Monday, Tuesday, and Wednesday.

On Wednesday, their area of North Dakota was supposed to get a big storm. People had been calling and canceling, shifting their appointments either earlier or later.

She needed to have groceries so she could ride out the storm, too.

The problem was, she needed money to buy groceries. She'd only had enough to get the absolute necessities last Thursday.

The extra bookings on the first three days of the week would be good for her pocketbook, although the lack of customers at the end of the week would more than make up for the abundance, she was sure.

"Ingrid," she said to her six-year-old, "Henry is spinning around in a circle. He's dizzy and can't control where he's going. Stand back away from him so he doesn't hit you."

She reached down and patted the top of her daughter's head as she clung to her leg, crying.

There were no red marks on her face and no new bumps that she could see. Ingrid had a tendency to be a bit dramatic.

Probably because she was a middle child who longed for attention.

The thought made Piper feel guilty. Was she not giving her kids enough attention?

She'd been assured by the ladies at church that it was perfectly normal for kids to want more attention than what their parents gave them. That middle children often developed ways of garnering attention for themselves, and it had nothing to do with Piper's lack of parenting skills.

She wanted to believe that, but it was hard.

Setting the empty box of pasta on the counter, she didn't stir it but knelt down, putting both arms around Ingrid.

"I think you're going to be okay. You can't cry every time someone touches you. Even if it hurts, a lot of times you have to just let it go. Especially if you know that you can go somewhere else in order to avoid being hit."

She hadn't been watching, didn't know for sure that Henry hadn't meant to hit Ingrid. But Ingrid was two years older than Henry was, and she was perfectly capable of getting out of his way.

"I'm hungry," Luna said beside her.

At two, almost three, Luna had really started to talk, and her favorite two words were "I'm hungry."

Theodora, who was almost two and who still hadn't grown enough hair to make her actually look like a girl so most people mistook her for a little boy, toddled over, seeing her mom kneeling down and wanting her fair share of attention, too.

Without really planning it, Piper ended up sitting on the floor, Ingrid on her lap, Luna and Theodora pushing in on either side, while Henry came running in, wanting to know where all of his playmates were, with Alice trailing behind.

It made for a lot of chaos in the kitchen, since the only one of her children who wasn't there was nine-year-old Lucas.

Sometimes she thought Lucas appreciated school just because he got to leave the chaos of his home and go someplace where things were a little more structured and calm.

That didn't mean that Lucas didn't love them or that he wouldn't do everything in his power to help his mom.

He was far too serious, since the death of her husband, almost two years ago.

Theodora had never met her father, since Piper had been pregnant with her at the time.

If she kept thinking about her late husband, she'd end up not only on the floor with all the kids on top of her, but crying as well.

"Guys, I need to stir the pasta. Or we won't have any lunch. It will all be stuck in a big goopy pile at the bottom of the pan."

Her kids didn't understand, at least Luna and Theodora didn't, and Ingrid still clung tightly to her neck.

She should have just shut the water off and planned on sitting on the floor and holding her kids for a little bit.

She had to work so much that she often didn't spend as much time with her kids as she wanted to.

She never scheduled clients on Sundays, and usually they went to church, when she could get herself dragged out of bed and get her kids ready in time.

Her husband, Richard, would have wanted her to take them.

She wanted to, too, just sometimes her want-tos didn't always equal her able-tos.

They sat like that until the water boiled over and started hissing on the stove.

The sound was enough to startle her children, which enabled her to scramble up, turning the heat down and grabbing a spoon to stir the sticking pasta.

It would be gluey but edible.

As she was setting the spoon down, she saw her phone light up with a text. She almost let it go, until a time with less chaos around her, but there really was never a time with less chaos, plus the fact that the storm was coming, and that a lot of clients were rescheduling, made her grab it and look.

> **If it's okay with you, I'm going to come out this afternoon and get started on the addition.**

She didn't recognize the number, but she didn't need to once she read the message. It was Gideon Marsh.

The chaos of her children playing wasn't quite as loud as it had been before she spent a few minutes on the floor with her kids, and her mind wandered as she walked to the cupboard and pulled out a jar of spaghetti sauce.

Gideon was coming.

She'd been hearing all last fall that he'd be coming to help put an addition onto her house. One she sorely needed, since she had her children divided into two bedrooms while she slept on the couch.

Before Richard died, he had been planning on adding on, but he intended to do most of the work himself and had been planning on taking on some extra jobs in order to pay for the lumber and materials.

Of course, after his death, that hadn't been something that was going to happen. Except the townspeople had rallied together and bought the materials.

Gideon had been supposed to do it last fall, but he had broken his leg and it had taken all winter to heal.

She assumed, since it was late March, that he would be starting whatever it was that he did with his friends on Sweet Briar Ranch soon. She knew they ran a crop-dusting service, plus she'd recently heard they were working on getting a dude ranch up. One of the perks of being a hairdresser was that she usually stayed up on all the local town news.

It seemed like the ex-Air Force dudes out on Sweet Briar Ranch were always busy with something, and she felt terrible that Mr. March, *Gideon*, was going to be taking time off to come put on her addition. Although, listening to the chaos in her kitchen and thinking about how nice it would be to have a little bit more space, she looked forward to it.

She appreciated it, truly.

Except...she didn't like the way she felt like she owed people who gave things to her, and if he spent most of the spring putting an addition on her house, she would owe him more than she could ever repay.

The ladies at church had told her over and over again that the Lord would take care of him and the Lord would eventually enable her to pass it on, but it still made her uncomfortable.

She'd never been someone who had needed charity before. And it didn't sit well with her.

It was her pride, she knew that.

Setting the jar of pasta sauce down and picking her phone back up, she sent a simple text.

Okay.

She wasn't going to fight, she wasn't going to argue, and she was going to try as hard as she could to be grateful.

His text came back right away.

Is one o'clock okay?

She glanced at the clock. 12:30. The kids would be done eating, easily. It didn't take them long at all. She might not have the mess cleaned up, but it didn't matter. The house was a disaster, with toys everywhere, blankets and pillows scattered around. The glass from the broken lamp had been cleaned up, but she'd moved the furniture out and not moved it back. The floor needed to be swept, and there was a huge stack of dishes in the sink.

She'd had clients until ten o'clock last night and hadn't done dishes for three days.

He might as well get to see what her house was going to typically look like while he was there.

It was just a pride thing that made her want to make it look different than it usually did.

Or maybe she wanted to put her best foot forward.

Not that she thought there was any chance of anything other than a very loose friendship between her and Gideon. It was just the idea that she didn't want to be pitied any more than she already was.

Maybe he wouldn't even notice the dirty house. Richard never had. He'd walked across her clean kitchen floor with mud on his shoes and never noticed that he was tracking it everywhere.

It irritated her, but it wasn't hard to forgive, or even overlook, because he had been such a good man. A good husband, a good father, but of course he wasn't perfect. She didn't expect him to be and wasn't going to complain about something simple like that, when he did so many other things exactly right.

Her heart gave a little squeeze at the thought, and she again pushed thoughts of Richard out of her head.

They had started dating about this time of year, and she supposed it was only natural that she thought about him a little more than what she normally did.

Grabbing her phone, she typed out one word.

Yes.

Pick up your copy of *Just a Cowboy's Shotgun Wedding* by Jessie Gussman today!

A Gift from Jessie

View this code through your smart phone camera to be taken to a page where you can download a FREE ebook when you sign up to get updates from Jessie Gussman! Find out why people say, "Jessie's is the only newsletter I open and read" and "You make my day brighter. Love, love, love reading your newsletters. I don't know where you find time to write books. You are so busy living life. A true blessing." and "I know from now on that I can't be drinking my morning coffee while reading your newsletter – I laughed so hard I sprayed it out all over the table!"

Claim your free book from Jessie!

Escape to more faith-filled romance series by Jessie Gussman!

The Complete Sweet Water, North Dakota Reading Order:
Series One: Sweet Water Ranch Western Cowboy Romance (11 book series)
Series Two: Coming Home to North Dakota (12 book series)
Series Three: Flyboys of Sweet Briar Ranch in North Dakota (13 book series)
Series Four: Sweet View Ranch Western Cowboy Romance (10 book series)

Spinoffs and More! Additional Series You'll Love:
Jessie's First Series: Sweet Haven Farm (4 book series)
Small-Town Romance: The Baxter Boys (5 book series)
Bad-Boy Sweet Romance: Richmond Rebels Sweet Romance (3 book series)
Sweet Water Spinoff: Cowboy Crossing (9 book series)
Holiday Romance: Cowboy Mountain Christmas (6 book series)
Small Town Romantic Comedy: Good Grief, Idaho (5 book series)
True Stories from Jessie's Farm: Stories from Jessie Gussman's Newsletter (3 book series)
Reader-Favorite! Sweet Beach Romance: Blueberry Beach (8 book series)
Cowboy Mountain Christmas Spinoff: A Heartland Cowboy Christmas (9 book series)
Blueberry Beach Spinoff: Strawberry Sands (10 book series)